MISTAKEN FOR A RAKE: A REGENCY ROMANCE
LANDON HOUSE (BOOK 1)

ROSE PEARSON

MISTAKEN FOR A RAKE

A REGENCY ROMANCE

Landon House

(Book 1)

By

Rose Pearson

© Copyright 2020 by Rose Pearson - All rights reserved.

In no way is it legal to reproduce, duplicate, or transmit any part of this document by either electronic means or in printed format. Recording of this publication is strictly prohibited and any storage of this document is not allowed unless with written permission from the publisher. All rights reserved.

Respective author owns all copyrights not held by the publisher.

CHAPTER ONE

"Do hurry up, Rebecca! The carriage has been waiting for some minutes and you are, again, tardy."

Rebecca bit her lip and forced herself not to retort words she would later regret back to her father. She would have liked to have told him the reason she was a little later than he expected was that she had spent some time sorting out a strong disagreement between her twin sisters, Anna and Selina. That had been a very lengthy discussion, and thus, she had been left with very little time of her own to prepare for this afternoon's outing.

"The carriage, the carriage!" the Duke said, ushering her in. "Your sisters are waiting!"

Smoothing her skirts as she sat, Rebecca looked at her sisters enquiringly, seeing the blush on both of their faces. They knew full well that the duke had been irritated with her when the fault was entirely their own. Of course, neither of them confessed, given that their father was already irritated and they did not want to incur his wrath.

A little frustrated, Rebecca turned her eyes to the window, hearing her father give instructions to the driver before he climbed into the carriage. She took a breath, letting it out slowly, dampening down her frustration.

"Now that we are *quite* ready," the Duke said, the door closed behind him, "perhaps we can finally be on our way to Madame Bernadotte." He sighed heavily. "You will have to be much more punctual from now on, Rebecca. From what I recall of London society, it is not at all acceptable to be late to soirees and dinner parties."

"Yes, Father," Rebecca replied monotonously. There was no excitement within her at the prospect of being a part of London society. Instead, there was the heavy burden of knowing that, most likely, she would have to guide her younger sisters through London in the hope that they would find suitable matches, for her father certainly would not do so. These last few years, her father had become more and more detached from his children, and Rebecca had been the one to step in where her father had failed.

Nothing would change now that they were in London, she was sure of it. He would expect her to do as she had always done. What hope did she have of finding a husband for herself when she had the responsibility of her twin sisters? It was just as well that the younger three remained at the estate in the care of their governess, else Rebecca did not know how she would have managed even to step outside the house!

"Rebecca?"

Turning her attention back to her father, Rebecca tried to smile. "Yes, Father?"

"Make sure that your sisters find what they require," he said vaguely. "I have no notion of fashion plates and the like. They will be guided by you."

Sighing inwardly and wishing that she knew what the fashion was to be this Season, she gave her father a brief nod and then returned her gaze to the window. This was going to be a very difficult Season indeed.

"Oh, I beg your pardon!"

Rebecca stumbled back, heat pouring into her cheeks as she realized that she had practically walked into another lady of the *ton* without realizing it. "Are you quite all right?"

The lady laughed and put one hand out towards Rebecca. "You need not worry, my dear," she said kindly, her blue eyes sparkling. "Are you going to Madame Bernadotte's?" She gestured to the establishment just ahead of Rebecca, her smile warm and friendly.

"Yes, yes, I am," Rebecca replied, still a little embarrassed. "My father..." She closed her eyes, then opened them, taking in a deep breath. "Forgive me." Dropping into a quick curtsy, she smiled back at the older lady. "If you would permit me to introduce myself, I am Lady Rebecca. My father is the Duke of Landon. He is presently inside with my two sisters, Lady Anna and Lady Selina."

"I see," the lady replied. "Then I do not think we should keep a duke waiting, Lady Rebecca. Shall we?"

A little surprised by the lady's forwardness, Rebecca

nodded and turned towards the door, all the more astonished when the lady followed after her.

"My son, it seems, has purchased me a pair of most expensive gloves," the lady continued with a wry smile. "He and I have come to London to speak to my late husband's solicitors about a few affairs. I think this gift is to encourage me to remain in London a little longer!"

Rebecca turned her head, lowering her voice as they walked inside. "I am sorry to hear of your husband's passing."

The lady smiled sadly, her expression now a little morose. "It was some years ago, Lady Rebecca, but I miss him still." She sighed softly, then gave herself a small shake. "But my son, the new Lord Hayward, has done very well in taking things on at the estate."

"I am glad to hear it," Rebecca replied, still feeling a trifle uncomfortable about the amount the lady was sharing when they had not been formally introduced. "I should go in search of my sisters now."

The lady's expression brightened. "But of course. Are you to have new gowns from Madame Bernadotte?"

Without meaning to, Rebecca allowed a heavy sigh to escape her, which, seeing the astonished look on Lady Hayward's face, only made a blush color her cheeks.

"Forgive me," she stammered, aware of her father's rumbling tones coming closer to her. "I did not mean to make any expression of complaint, Lady Hayward. It is only that, given that my mother is no longer with us, I have been given the responsibility of ensuring that my sisters and I are dressed appropriately. If I am truthful, I do not know precisely what would be best." She shrugged, heat still pouring into her face. "We have never been to London, and I do not know much about society." Quite why she was expressing this much to a lady she had never met before in her life, Rebecca could not explain, but there was something in the lady's expression that was so welcoming and encouraging that she felt as though she could tell her anything.

Lady Hayward tilted her head, her eyes considering. "I would be happy to assist you in this, Lady Rebecca," she said slowly. "I am aware that we have only just met, but if you have no other friends within London as yet to aid you, then I would be glad to offer my assistance."

"Assistance?"

Rebecca closed her eyes briefly, hearing the note of confusion in her father's voice.

"Father," she said quickly, turning to face the duke and seeing how his green eyes—so akin to her own—were watching Lady Hayward with something like suspicion. "This is Lady Hayward. She and I were quickly introduced as we came into this establishment. She is, very kindly, offering to do what she can to ensure that my sisters and I choose gowns of the highest fashion." Smiling quickly, she gestured to Lady Hayward. "Lady Hayward, forgive my improper manner. I should have introduced you properly." Praying that the lady did not think her entirely unsuitable for being anywhere near London, she tried again. "Might I present my father, the Duke of Landon."

Lady Hayward curtsied quickly, although she did not show any sign of awe or astonishment at being in the presence of a duke, as Rebecca had seen so many visitors do when they had come to the estate. "Good afternoon, Your Grace. I am very glad to meet you. As Lady Rebecca had just informed you, I would be glad to assist her with the ordering of suitable gowns for this Season." She smiled, and Rebecca saw the way the frown began to lift from her father's face. "In truth, it can be quite a burdensome task!"

Rebecca held her breath for a few moments, looking towards her father and entirely uncertain as to what his reaction might be. She prayed that he would be willing to permit Lady Hayward to do as she had offered for, whilst Rebecca had only just met the lady, she was certain that any assistance she could receive at this present juncture would be most appreciated.

The duke harrumphed for a moment, his gaze turning towards Rebecca, who continued to watch him hopefully.

"Very well," he said, speaking slowly as though he was not quite certain that such a thing was appropriate, his brow furrowing as he looked back towards Lady Hayward. "But only if it does not delay you, Lady Hayward."

Lady Hayward laughed and shook her head. "No, it does not," she replied with a smile. "In truth, I would be glad for the distraction! I have very little else to occupy me at present." Turning her head, she smiled at Rebecca, who, with relief, smiled back. "Might you introduce me to your sisters, Lady Rebecca? I should be glad to meet them."

"But of course," Rebecca said quickly, putting one

hand on her father's arm. "Father, if you wish to wait, then might I suggest—"

"I would be glad to chaperone your daughters, Your Grace, if that would be of assistance."

Rebecca stared at Lady Hayward as she not only interrupted Rebecca but spoke with such a boldness that Rebecca herself was caught by surprise.

"As I have said, I have nothing else to occupy me at present and choosing gowns can take many hours," Lady Hayward continued, her eyes dancing as the duke's frown deepened at the obvious displeasure that came with knowing he would be forced to remain at Madame Bernadotte's for some time. "My carriage is only just outside, and I would be glad to return them to the house when we are finished here."

"How very good of you, Lady Hayward," the duke said, inclining his head just a little. "I confess that I am somewhat out of my depth when it comes to what my daughters require." His eyes studied the lady for a few seconds before he nodded. "It would be a great help to me if you would do as you have suggested, Lady Hayward. That would mean that I could continue with particular matters of business that require my attention." A slight narrowing of his eyes betrayed his flickering uncertainty. "But are you quite certain that you have nothing else to occupy you this afternoon? I should not like to take advantage."

Rebecca feared that Lady Hayward would take offense at this clear disbelief, for it was more than apparent that the Duke was not at all certain that Lady

Hayward spoke the truth, but much to her relief, the lady in question did not appear at all perturbed.

"Your Grace, as I was telling your daughter only a few minutes before, my son, Lord Hayward, has purchased me a pair of gloves from Madame Bernadotte's, which I am now to collect. Thereafter, I have nothing at all to engage me for, like you, my son has matters of business to attend to."

"And you have no daughters?"

"I do," Lady Hayward replied, her expression gentling as she thought of the young lady, "but she is not yet out and remains at the estate. I am here in London with my eldest son in the hope of resolving a few matters of business. I will return home soon, of course, but not before such things are settled."

Hearing the two voices of her sisters echoing through the establishment, Rebecca turned a pleading gaze towards her father. "Might I take Lady Hayward to my sisters, Father?" she asked, but the Duke did not so much as glance at her. Rather, he fixed his gaze upon Lady Hayward, his eyes thoughtful as a look of interest drew into his expression.

"You are very kind to offer such a thing, Lady Hayward," he said slowly, choosing each word with care. "I would be in your debt, should you be willing to bring my daughters home once their gowns have been ordered. However, I wonder if I might, thereafter, ask if you would be willing to speak with me at greater length once you have returned them to the house." He looked at the lady steadily, and a swirl of anxiety swept through Rebecca's frame. What was it her father was doing? And what was it he wanted? She could not imagine what he intended to say to Lady Hayward, and, from the way the smile was beginning to fade from Lady Hayward's expression, it seemed that she could not either.

"If you wish it, Your Grace," Lady Hayward replied, a line forming between her brows as she watched the Duke, seemingly intent on deriving his wishes a little better by studying him. "I will, of course, do as you ask."

The Duke smiled suddenly, a light coming into his eyes that had not been there before. It was as though Lady Hayward's agreement had brought a sense of delight to him, although still, Rebecca did not know what to make of it all.

"Excellent, excellent!" the duke exclaimed before turning back to Rebecca, one hand on her shoulder. "Now, Rebecca, you shall make certain that your sisters behave with all propriety. They must make an excellent impression here in London, even within the dressmaker's!"

"Yes, Father," Rebecca murmured, her gaze sliding towards Lady Hayward, who was, she noted, watching the Duke with interest. "I will, of course, do as you ask."

"Wonderful," the Duke replied, seemingly now very relieved that he would be freed of the burden of his daughters. "I shall return to the townhouse, then. Make certain to do all that Lady Hayward asks and listen to her advice." His hand lifted from her shoulder, but the familiar weight of responsibility immediately came. "And, of course, there is no need to concern yourself with the cost of such gowns, Rebecca. Choose whatever you wish and whatever is needed and have the bill sent directly."

"Yes, Father," Rebecca murmured, dropping her head as warmth entered her cheeks. She wished he would not speak of his wealth in such terms, not when Lady Hayward was present. It was, she considered, a little uncouth and ill-considered but, given that her father was not likely to listen to any word she had to say on the matter, Rebecca remained entirely silent.

"Capital!" the Duke boomed before bidding a quick farewell to both Rebecca and Lady Hayward and then making his way to the door. A tight band released itself slowly from Rebecca's chest as she heard the bell tinkle above the door of the shop, signaling that her father had left. A small sigh left her lips as she looked at Lady Hayward, who was watching her with a good deal of curiosity.

"I should introduce you to my sisters at once," Rebecca found herself saying, a little unnerved by the watchfulness in the lady's expression. "I—"

"You are often given responsibility for your sisters, I think," Lady Hayward said quietly. "Is that not so, Lady Rebecca?"

"It is, yes," Rebecca agreed, choosing not to hold back the truth from Lady Hayward. "My mother passed away when my youngest sister was only a babe. Since then, I have been given much of the responsibility of raising them and guiding them, although, of course, we have had governesses and the like." She tried to smile but found she could not, feeling as though she was unburdening her very soul for what would be the first time. "The three youngest are still at my father's estate, and, whilst I believe my father expects me to make a match this Season, I confess that I am not at all hopeful."

"Because you must seek out what is best for your sisters," Lady Hayward replied, clearly understanding everything Rebecca was saying without her having to express it directly. "Well, Lady Rebecca, mayhap that might change somewhat. Perhaps there is more I can do to aid you in this so that you have the opportunity yourself to find a suitable husband."

Rebecca's mouth lifted into a small, sad smile. "You are very kind, Lady Hayward," she said quietly, feeling as though she had known the lady for a good deal longer than only a few short minutes. "I will gladly welcome whatever it is you wish to offer."

Lady Haywood laughed softly, then gestured to someone or something over Rebecca's shoulder. "Perhaps we should start with the introduction of your sisters," she said as Rebecca turned around to see her sister, Lady Anna, standing only a short distance away, with something in her hands. "And then we must speak to Madame Bernadotte herself, to see what she requires of you all. No doubt, there will be measurements taken before we even consider what colors would best suit."

Rebecca felt the heavy burden of responsibility lift just a little as she turned around to lead Lady Hayward towards her sisters. This afternoon, at least, she would not be solely responsible for the gowns her sisters chose, the gowns that they would wear into society. She had Lady Hayward's experience and understanding now, even though they were only very briefly acquainted. For whatever reason, Rebecca felt as though she had found a caring and concerned individual whose eagerness to help came from a place of true kindness, and for that, she found herself increasingly grateful.

"Anna," she said, seeing her other sister standing a short distance away. "And Selina, might you join us for a moment?" Waiting until both had joined them, Rebecca turned to Lady Hayward. "Lady Hayward, might I present my two sisters." She gestured to the first. "This is Lady Anna, and next to her, Lady Selina."

Lady Hayward curtsied. "I am glad to make your acquaintance."

"And this is Lady Hayward," Rebecca told her sisters, who were both looking at her with a mixture of confusion and interest. "Father has returned to the townhouse and has left Lady Hayward to assist us in choosing our gowns. We will return with her once we are finished here."

Her sisters' eyes widened in evident surprise, but Anna was the first one to speak, excited tones pouring from her mouth as she engaged Lady Hayward in conversation almost at once. She spoke about colors and gloves and ribbons, begging Lady Hayward to join her so that she might show her what she had been considering. Rebecca smiled to herself, thinking that it was very much like Anna to be so eager, whilst Selina, as she expected, stayed back just a little, watching carefully but having none of the enthusiasm of her twin sister.

"You have only just met Lady Hayward, then?" Lady Selina asked as Rebecca nodded. "And Father is quite contented to allow her to help us?"

"*More* than willing, I should say," Rebecca replied

with a sudden smile. "In fact, I do not think he was hesitant for barely a moment! The opportunity to return to the townhouse and to remove himself from supervising the choosing of gowns was one he could not simply ignore." She chuckled, and, finally, Lady Selina smiled. "I think we may have found an ally in Lady Hayward, Selina." A jolt of happiness ran through her frame, and Rebecca allowed herself to sigh with contentment. "Perhaps this Season will not be as difficult as I feared after all."

CHAPTER TWO

"I do hope there will be no tardiness this evening!"

Rebecca sat up straight in her chair as her father came striding into the room, only to stop dead as he caught sight of not one but three of his daughters sitting quietly together, waiting for him to join them. He cleared his throat and nodded at them, muttering something under his breath that Rebecca could not quite make out.

Rebecca felt delighted with his reaction, but, of course, hid it well. It would not do to have her father irritated just before they left the house for what would be their very first foray into society.

"Now that you have been presented," the Duke said, coming to stand in front of the small fire that burned in the grate, keeping the evening's chill away from the large room, "it is time to enter society. You are, however, to be on your guard."

Rebecca frowned. "If you are to suggest, Father, that we do not know what is expected of us in terms of behavior, then—"

"That is not at all what I am suggesting, Rebecca, and kindly do not interrupt," the duke said firmly, his eyes fixing to hers as she quelled her frustration. "I am well aware that my daughters know what is proper and what is improper. I fully expect this evening to go very well, indeed. What I am to say, however, is that you all must be careful of those you are introduced to. Some will be eager for your acquaintance, of course, which will be rather flattering." His lips thinned, giving Rebecca the impression that he had been through an experience that had not pleased him. "It will be a matter of wisdom and consideration to know whether such people are eager for your acquaintance out of an eagerness to become known to you, or if they seek it out for their own gain."

Rebecca's heart began to grow heavy. She had been looking forward to this evening, especially with the promise of Lady Hayward being present also. The purchasing of their gowns had gone very well indeed and, whilst Rebecca did not know what Lady Hayward and her father had discussed thereafter, she felt quite certain that the duke would be very contented indeed with their acquaintance continuing. Now, however, she feared that her father would expect her to ensure that her sisters were acquainted only with those that were of excellent character and had no underlying motives—although quite how she was meant to decipher such a thing, Rebecca had very little idea.

"Therefore, you must be on your guard," the duke said firmly. "If, for any reason, a gentleman is eager to further his acquaintance with you, you shall give his name to me, and I shall do some investigation into his situation before any further interaction takes place."

"Yes, Father," the three young ladies murmured together, with Rebecca's heart sinking all the lower. She would never be able to find a suitable match, not when her father's demands were so stringent. What if she found someone she considered appropriate, only for her father to refuse on some small matter? She knew that the duke expected his daughters to marry well, to gentlemen of excellent title, of good family, and of substantial wealth. Now, it seemed, she had to find such a gentleman but would also be required to ensure that his character was without fault and his motivations quite pure. It felt like a near-impossible task.

The duke cleared his throat, his hands still clasped tightly behind his back, and Rebecca forced herself to give him her full attention and did not linger on any further thoughts at present.

"There is another matter that I wish to inform you of," the duke continued as Rebecca let out a long, slow breath, a little frustrated that there appeared to be even more the duke required of them. "It is to do with Lady Hayward."

Rebecca's heart dropped to the floor. No doubt, then, the duke had found something disparaging about the lady and had decided that she was not a suitable acquaintance for his daughters. Perhaps that was what had been discussed yesterday afternoon when they had returned from Madame Bernadotte's. Perhaps Lady Hayward had been thanked by the duke but asked to remove herself from their acquaintance. It was quite feasible, given all that the duke expected, and yet Rebecca felt sorrowful, having thought very highly of Lady Hayward.

"As you know, Lady Hayward is a kind and willing lady who has very little to occupy her at present," the duke began, his voice rolling through the room. "I was grateful to her for her assistance yesterday, and I am sure that, given how highly you all spoke of her, you were grateful for her company also."

"We were, Father," Lady Anna replied quietly. "I believe we all thought very highly of her."

"Good." The duke paused for a moment and, much to Rebecca's astonishment, began to smile. What was it he was going to reveal? She was no longer as certain as she had been about her father's intentions, praying that he would not ask them to separate from the lady entirely.

"Lady Hayward has a son. Three, in fact," the duke continued, now looking pleased with himself. "There are a few issues concerning the late Lord Hayward's will, and, in addition, I believe the new Lord Hayward is struggling just a little with all that has been placed upon his shoulders." He shrugged. "It is understandable when one takes the title to be a little overwhelmed, but there are certain matters that make things a good deal more difficult for Lord Hayward. Therefore, having discussed the matter at length with Lady Hayward, she and I have come to a mutually agreed arrangement."

A flurry of either fear or excitement—for Rebecca could not tell which—ran down her spine as she listened intently, wondering what it could be that had been agreed upon. It was not like her father to go about such things in this way, for he did not like to ask anyone for their help or assistance in anything, being quite determined to do it without interference. And yet, in this case, it appeared as though this was precisely what he had done.

"I have no interest in attending balls, in encouraging matches and in chaperoning waltzes and the like," the duke said with a wave of his hand and a sigh of exasperation. "Lady Hayward has no real interest in business matters, although, of course, she wishes to aid her son in any way she can. Therefore, we have both agreed to be of assistance to the other."

Silence filled the room for a few minutes as the three ladies looked at their father expectantly, clearly ready for him to say more, but it seemed as though the duke was finished with his explanations. With a shrug, he turned and gestured to the door. "Let us hurry now. She will be waiting."

Rebecca did not move from her chair. "What do you mean, Father?" she asked as Lady Anna and Lady Selina watched the duke with curiosity. "Lady Hayward is to assist you? In what way?"

"By chaperoning you, of course," he said, a slight flicker crossing his brow as though he had expected them all to understand what he meant without difficulty. "She will do what I do not wish to and will guide you through society and make certain that any gentlemen who wish to acquaint themselves a little more with you are entirely suitable."

Lady Selina spoke up. "And you will be with us also?"

"For heavens' sake, Selina!" The duke threw up his

hands, clearly exasperated. "Do you have no understanding at all? No, I shall *not* be with you. Lady Hayward will go in my place as your chaperone. In return, I am to assist her son with his present difficulties and, thereafter, look to the future of the two younger sons also." He smiled suddenly, his face alight with eagerness. "She will be glad to help each of my daughters, it seems, which means I shall have very little to do with London society," he finished, evidently very relieved indeed that he should not have to go about within it. "I can remain focused on matters at hand and, when the time comes, settle an excellent dowry for each of my daughters."

Rebecca did not know what to say in response to this. On one hand, she wanted to tell her father that she found his lack of willingness and even eagerness to help his daughters navigate society to be a little disheartening. But on the other hand, she found herself very pleased indeed to be relieved of the burden of leading her sisters in London society. The duke would not need her to step into her familiar role; she would be free of that entirely! She might, perhaps, have the opportunity to take on society as she had always dreamed of!

"What say you, Rebecca?"

She looked up at her father, wondering if he had known that she struggled with varying emotions, for mayhap they had been displayed across her face.

"I think it will suit us all very well," she said calmly, making certain not to give voice to any of her thoughts regarding her father's behavior. As much as she might wish him to be a little more involved in their lives, as much as she might hope for a certain amount of change,

Rebecca realized that such a thing would never be. Her father had his way of dealing with his daughters and, as such, would never be to her what she had always hoped.

"And you, Selina? Anna?"

Both of them nodded their agreement and glanced toward Rebecca as though they were not entirely sure of her reaction. When the duke announced that they were ready to depart and that there was no more need to linger, Rebecca rose quickly from her chair, now all the more eager to make her way to the ball.

"You are contented with this, Rebecca?" Anna asked as Rebecca moved towards the door. "Do you think that Lady Hayward will be a helpful chaperone?"

"The lady is *more* than capable, and I think we should be grateful for her help," Rebecca replied firmly. "It may not be what we were expecting, but I, for one, am profoundly glad to know that it will not be my duty to ensure you are both doing well this Season. I shall be able to have the freedom that I was not expecting."

This did not seem to make much of an impression upon Anna, for she merely nodded and looked away, perhaps not fully understanding all that Rebecca was burdened by. Letting out a long breath, Rebecca allowed herself to become excited at the prospect of stepping out into society for the first time.

She was, of course, aware that a duke's daughter would be very much sought after by some gentlemen, given that she had an excellent dowry and title, but Rebecca was determined to be careful in her judgments. It was not that she expected any sort of affection from either herself or her future husband, but preferred to consider all the practical requirements that would be necessary. Her father would have to be satisfied with the fellow entirely before he would permit even a courtship, so it would be wise for Rebecca to choose sensibly rather than throw her heart open to all manner of emotion.

"Then to the ball we are to go!" the duke declared as Rebecca sat down quickly beside her sisters, clasping her hands in her lap as her excitement grew. "And my daughters are to make a wonderful first impression upon the *beau monde*, I am sure of it."

"Thank you for your confidence in us, Father," Rebecca replied as her other two sisters murmured the same. "We will not let you down."

"No, no, of course, you will not," he replied with such warmth in his voice that Rebecca was surprised. "You have done very well, Rebecca, in all things."

She did not know what to say, his compliment sending a wave of happiness into her heart— happiness she had not felt in some time.

"Thank you, Father," she said again, her voice a little quieter than before. "That is very kind of you."

He cleared his throat, mayhap a little embarrassed. "Yes, well, you shall have all the more success with Lady Hayward. I am very glad that such an arrangement has been made." Taking in a breath, he let it out slowly. "I will, of course, be present this evening with you, but thereafter, Lady Hayward will be your chaperone. From time to time, I might attend if there is to be a card game or the like—something that I am interested in—but besides that, I shall either remain at the townhouse or be otherwise engaged."

"Of course, Father," Selina said quietly, her voice barely loud enough to hear over the noise of the carriage wheels. "We quite understand."

"Good!" the duke exclaimed as the carriage began to slow. "Then let us hope this evening is the success I expect it to be!"

"Good evening, Lady Hayward."

The lady smiled up at the duke for a moment before curtsying. "Good evening, Your Grace," she replied before turning to the sisters. "And good evening to you all also."

Rebecca smiled back at Lady Hayward, bobbing a quick curtsy. "Good evening, Lady Hayward," she answered. "Father has told us of the arrangement between you."

"I hope that is satisfactory to you," Lady Hayward said, her smile fading a little. "I have many acquaintances here in London mostly due to my late husband's connections. They have children of their own, many of whom are present here in London and seeking a match, just as you are. I am sure that I can guide you to a good number of acquaintances."

"We are all very eager to come under your chaperonage," Rebecca replied, aware of the flash of relief that hurried into Lady Hayward's eyes. "You are very kind, Lady Hayward."

This seemed to please the lady all the more, for she blushed and waved a hand.

"It is my pleasure and certainly not something I am doing without recompense!" she laughed, her brightness returning in an instant. "I am very grateful to His Grace for being so willing to help my son."

The Duke waved his hand. "Very well, very well," he said hastily as though he did not want to make mention of what had been agreed between himself and Lady Hayward. "Now, I shall take Lady Anna and Lady Selina with me for a short turn around the room. I am certain I will meet a few acquaintances to whom I might introduce them." He looked to Rebecca. "You might go with Lady Hayward, Rebecca."

A little surprised, Rebecca quickly recovered herself and nodded. "Yes, of course, Father," she said as Lady Hayward nodded her agreement. "At once."

Quickly, Anna and Selina followed after their father, who had turned away from Lady Hayward in an instant, clearly decisive in his actions. Rebecca, still a little surprised, waited for Lady Hayward to step forward before she turned to join her.

They walked quietly together for a few moments, and Rebecca found herself a little uncertain of what to say. This had been thrust upon them quickly, and, whilst she was very glad indeed of both Lady Hayward's company and her willingness to help, she was not quite sure what there was next to do.

"I presume that your father did not inform you of this arrangement until this evening," Lady Hayward said, looking at Rebecca with a twinkle in her eye. "You all appear to be a little overwhelmed."

"I am a little," Rebecca admitted, finding herself

relaxing even as she spoke. "Yes, you are quite correct, Lady Hayward. He told us in the few minutes we had before we left the house. Although I will say that I am very grateful to you."

"Oh?" Lady Hayward looked a little surprised. "I am certain you would have done very well under your father's guidance, Lady Rebecca."

An answer came to her lips, but Rebecca hesitated, not quite certain whether or not she ought to speak the truth of what was on her heart for fear that she might say ill of her father. Lady Hayward did not encourage her to say a word, however, but continued walking quietly and slowly, looking all about her at the other guests.

"Ever since my mother passed, I have felt a heavy burden for my sisters," she explained. "That did not fade when it came to the Season." She glanced at Lady Hayward, who, whilst listening, did not appear to have any expression of judgment on her face. "I fully expected to have to chaperone my sisters and ensure that they met suitable gentlemen rather than being able to pursue such a thing myself."

"I understand," Lady Hayward replied gently. "You need not explain further, Lady Rebecca. I am, however, all the more happy to be of help to you. As you are the eldest, it is only right that you should find a match first, although I applaud your willingness to help your sisters in such a way."

A flush of embarrassment caught Rebecca's cheeks. "I am not worthy of such accolades," she replied, a little ashamed. "I have spent many moments complaining and becoming frustrated with my responsibilities, rather than accepting what has been."

"That is not something I shall hold against you," Lady Hayward answered firmly. "Now, Lady Rebecca, tell me of the sort of gentleman that you would be glad to consider as a suitable husband."

Rebecca's flush only deepened, but Lady Hayward laughed and pressed her to speak openly.

"I have given it *some* consideration," Rebecca replied eventually, hating that her cheeks were so colored. "He would have to have an excellent title. I believe a marquess would be the most acceptable to my father. In addition, he must be solvent, of course, with no penchant for wasting it away on something such as gambling or horseflesh. I believe my father would be expecting that he would have a large estate, with evidence of profit from each year, as well as a plan for how the estate might continue to grow and flourish." She lifted one shoulder, allowing herself to look out at the various gentlemen who were moving past them, wondering which one might have such qualities. "He would have to be sensible, not prone to drunkenness, and be eager to produce an heir. That is all I believe that my father would expect."

Relieved that she had spoken as Lady Hayward had wished, Rebecca turned her head to her chaperone, wondering what the lady would make of it, only to see her gazing back at Rebecca with utter astonishment. Her blue eyes were wide, her mouth a little ajar, and had come to a complete halt, staring at Rebecca as though she had gone quite mad.

"Did I say something upsetting?" Rebecca asked, now

all the more embarrassed at such a reaction from the lady. "I apologize if I—"

"My dear Lady Rebecca!" Lady Hayward exclaimed, grasping Rebecca's hand suddenly and shaking her head with such fervor that, for a moment, Rebecca feared that the lady was unwell. "What can you be thinking of?"

"I—I do not understand what you mean," Rebecca replied, stammering just a little. "I have only spoken as you asked me."

"No, no!" Lady Hayward exclaimed, a now considerate smile spreading across her face. "There must be more to your expectations of a husband than that, Lady Rebecca!" Lowering her voice and still holding Rebecca's hand, she took a small step closer. "When I ask you about what you are considering in terms of suitable gentlemen, I do not mean what requirements fulfill your father's satisfaction, Lady Rebecca, but what *you* consider!"

Rebecca shook her head. "I do not know what you mean, Lady Hayward."

Lady Hayward pressed her fingers gently and then removed her hand. "Should you like him to be kind? Considerate? Would you like a husband who would make you smile? Shall he enjoy horse riding, for example, if that is something you enjoy? What shared interests might you have? Should you prefer a gentleman bold and loud or quiet and a little more studious?" Her eyes sparkled. "And there is always the consideration as to whether or not the gentleman's features are appealing to you, Lady Rebecca. That is not something that ought to be ignored. One should not marry a gentleman that does not have a handsome quality about him, although that particular preference changes from person to person."

Rebecca, who had never heard anyone speak in such a frank way before nor had ever even *thought* of such a thing before, did not know what to say. She swallowed hard, her cheeks burning hot, and her mind whirling with all manner of thoughts.

"I can see that we will have to have many discussions before we can settle on a particular sort of gentleman," Lady Hayward said, no mockery in her voice but with a gentleness in her manner that took away some of Rebecca's embarrassment. "It is not something you have considered, then?"

"No," Rebecca replied, hoarsely. "I have never once permitted myself to think of anything other than what my father will require."

"Well, you shall do so now," Lady Hayward answered decisively. "I shall introduce you to various gentlemen this evening, Lady Rebecca, and perhaps tomorrow, you and I shall discuss their merits and whether or not you had any particular interest in any one of them."

This sounded quite a horrifying prospect to Rebecca, who had never even thought that such a thing would take place. When thinking of the coming Season, she had supposed that she would meet a gentleman who seemed to be suitable, would mention his name to her father, and that, thereafter, a match would be made. And, if the gentleman was not found to be all that her father required, then she would consider another. Never once had she thought about what she herself would seek! But now Lady Hayward was quite convinced that she ought to do so, and Rebecca did not know what to think.

"Let us begin with the Marquess of Lancaster," Lady Hayward said practically, looping her hand through Rebecca's arm. "And thereafter, perhaps the Earl of Bridgewater?" A laugh escaped her as she looked up into Rebecca's startled face. "Have no fear, Lady Rebecca. All will be well, although perhaps a little altered from what you had anticipated."

"Yes, very different indeed," Rebecca replied, lifting her chin and forcing air into her tight lungs. She would allow Lady Hayward to be her guide and, in doing so, would make herself consider things she had not before. Rebecca could only pray, however, that she would not make a fool of herself but would instead make an excellent impression upon society that her father expected. She could do nothing less than that.

CHAPTER THREE

With a small sigh, Jeffery stepped into the ballroom and looked all about him. He was not particularly enamored with society, but with very little else to entertain him back at his estate, he had decided to return to London to partake of London's diversions.

"Good evening, Lord Richmond."

"Good evening," he murmured, bowing low towards Lady Kensington, who had floated towards him almost the moment he had entered the drawing-room. "I thank you for your invitation this evening, Lady Kensington. I do apologize for my tardiness." Looking about him, he tried to find Lord Kensington but could not see him anywhere. "I should like to greet your husband also."

Lady Kensington trilled a laugh and, much to Jeffery's discomfort, trailed one hand down his arm. He did not remove himself from her presence, however, knowing that to do so would appear very rude indeed, even though he did not appreciate her gesture. Her dress seemed to be the latest stare of fashion, and the neckline was quite low to show off her charms. Jeffery, however, avoided looking at her bosom as he did not want to encourage her attentions.

"He is already deep in conversation about some matter of importance, Lord Richmond," Lady Kensington told him, her eyes now practically fixed to his own, her fingers brushing down his hand. "A very *dull* matter, however." She sighed plaintively, then snapped her fingers towards one of the footmen, who brought over his tray at once, allowing Jeffery to pick up a glass of brandy as Lady Kensington continued to watch him. The urge to remove himself from her company grew within him, but Jeffery knew he could not do so, not without making himself appear very rude indeed. For whatever reason, Lady Kensington had been overfamiliar during last year's Season, and she now appeared to be behaving in much the same way—much to Jeffery's frustration.

"Again, forgive my tardiness," he said, struggling to find what else to say. "I was, I am afraid, caught up in a matter that could not be set aside."

"But it is resolved now, I hope?" she asked, her eyes a little wider than before as she looked up at him. "You will not have to depart early?"

"No, no, indeed not," he replied as a bright smile broke out across her face. "I shall be very happy to remain here this evening, Lady Kensington. Now," he cleared his throat and inclined his head. "If you will excuse me, I should greet your husband, even if he is caught up in an important discussion. I must beg pardon for my late arrival."

Lady Kensington let out a murmur of protest, but

Jeffery quickly took his leave of her, a slight shiver running down his spine as he glanced back over his shoulder to see Lady Kensington still watching him, her eyes glittering darkly. She was, of course, a very beautiful lady, but Jeffery was not the sort of gentleman to chase after another man's wife, no matter how much she batted her lashes at him.

"It seems Lady Kensington is just as eager as before, then."

Jeffery gave his friend a tight smile, a deeply unsettling feeling in his stomach. "Indeed," he muttered as Lord Swinton shook his head in a manner that spoke of his dislike of Lady Kensington's behavior. "You behave in a most admirable fashion, Richmond. Many gentlemen would have given in to her. In fact, I am quite certain that many *have* done so."

Taking a sip of his brandy, Jeffery drew in a long breath. "I am not one of them," he muttered as Lord Swinton grinned. "As much as she might wish it, I am not at all inclined towards her."

"And we are all aware of it," Lord Swinton replied, slapping Jeffery on the shoulder. "Now that I consider it, you have not shown any interest in any lady whatsoever, save for that one debutante some two Seasons ago!"

It was something of a painful memory and not one that Jeffery relished being brought back to his attention. "If you are speaking of Miss St. Claire, then I can assure you that there was no *real* interest there," he lied. "And when she chose another, I was quite happy."

Lord Swinton laughed and shook his head. "I will not believe that, no matter how often you try to convince me of it," he said with a grin. "You had your heart quite broken and since then have been unable to find another young lady that can in any way compare to Miss St. Claire."

"Enough," Jeffery growled, having had his fill of Lord Swinton's jibes. "If you recall, we were discussing Lady Kensington." He kept his voice low, not wanting anyone to overhear him. "Is there any advice you wish to give me, Swinton? Or will you merely continue to mock me?"

Lord Swinton did not immediately answer, his expression becoming a little more serious as he tilted his head and let his gaze flick back towards Lady Kensington, who was, Jeffery presumed, still standing somewhere behind him.

"I have no advice to give you," Lord Swinton said eventually as Jeffery let out a heavy sigh of frustration. "You can continue to push aside her attentions as you have been doing, but other than that, I cannot see what you can do."

"Do you think Lord Kensington is aware of her... eagerness?" Jeffery asked, a little anxious that he might find himself in a little difficulty should Lord Kensington notice his wife's behavior. "If he is, then I am not at all sure what I ought to do."

Lord Swinton shook his head. "The man either is fully aware of her and chooses to ignore it, or he is a simpleton," he said bluntly. "I am more inclined to lean towards the first suggestion, however. I am sure that is why he is so often absent at events such as this or, at the very least, standing separately from his wife."

Jeffery winced. "That must be most unfortunate for him."

"That," Lord Swinton replied sharply, "is because he was foolish enough to marry a young lady that was both much too young for his older years and much too silly for his sensible nature. He ought to have made a match with more consideration than he did. Little wonder that his wife now seeks out better company than he, for they are so mismatched that she must be very bored indeed!"

A murmur of protest in Jeffery's heart brought a quick response. "I do not think that either a difference in years nor in nature is enough of an excuse to behave in such a way," he replied as Lord Swinton shrugged. "I should expect a lady such as she to be flirtatious, yes, but to be so overt and intentional that everyone within the *ton* sees it is quite another thing."

"Again," Lord Swinton replied, "it is to be expected with such a silly creature as she." He laughed and slapped Jeffery on the shoulder again. "You are much too proper, Richmond: that is your only foible," he chuckled as Jeffery shrugged him off. "Most other gentlemen would accept Lady Kensington's attentions without hesitation, whereas you are quite determined not to do so."

"Because it would not be right," Jeffery replied, now a little irritated by his friend's remark as well as his broad smile. "Now, where is Lord Kensington? I must go and greet him at once."

Lord Swinton looked all about him and then shrugged. "I could not say," he remarked. "You know how the gentleman is. Most likely, he will have dragged one of his guests to his study to review some dull papers of some sort. He loves his investments more than he loves these balls."

"Perhaps," Jeffery replied with a sigh before finishing off the rest of his brandy. "Well, if he is not here at present, then I should greet a few others before, as I presume it shall be, we are requested to listen to a few of the young ladies perform for our listening pleasure." He chuckled at the grimace that appeared in an instant upon Lord Swinton's face. "A favorite of yours, I think."

"Mayhap I shall have to suggest a game of cards or the like, so that I will be excused from having to give them the entirety of my concentration," Lord Swinton muttered, no longer grinning as he had done. "But yes, be off with you. There are bound to be a few young ladies eager to make your acquaintance!"

Jeffery laughed and then walked away, quickly spying another group of gentlemen—with one or two ladies present also—where he might make conversation. Thus, the evening went pleasantly enough and, when it grew near to the time for the music to begin and the entertainment to start, Jeffery found himself enjoying the spirit of the evening. He had forgotten entirely about Lady Kensington's advances and had been enjoying an excellent conversation with another gentleman, as well as being introduced to a few lovely young ladies. All in all, it had been an excellent evening thus far, and he was looking forward to what came thereafter, even if Lord Swinton was not!

"Lord Richmond! I have only just discovered the whereabouts of my husband." Lady Kensington came to stand directly in front of him, preventing him from taking a step further, and Jeffery was forced to stand before her as though he were the subject and she the ruler. "I know that you have not greeted him as yet and that you do very much wish to do so, and thus, I have made every effort to satisfy such a whim." She laughed brightly and settled a hand on his arm. "He is in the study at present, with Lord Millerton, whom, I am sure, would be glad for a little relief."

Jeffery hesitated. "I see. I should not like to step away from this evening's entertainment, however," he said. "Will your husband be joining us for that?"

Lady Kensington shrugged and looked away. "Who can tell?" she replied somewhat morosely. "I had thought he would attempt to be the host the *beau monde* expects, but it seems that, yet again, I am mistaken."

Something tugged in Jeffery's heart as he watched Lady Kensington. Despite her marked flirtations, there was, he considered, a small flicker of genuine frustration in her voice and her demeanor at present. It was clear that she did, in fact, find Lord Kensington's absence to be something of an embarrassment, clearly aware that the *ton* considered him a less-than-suitable host who very often neglected his duties towards his guests. Even Jeffery knew of it, but it had never once stopped him from attending.

"Might you not send a footman to fetch him?" he asked doubtfully, but Lady Kensington quickly shook her head, a false brightness about her now as she suddenly took hold of the situation in place of her husband.

"Ladies and gentlemen," she said, her voice filling the room. "Please, if you would come through, we might sit together for a short while as we are entertained by some of the most wonderfully talented young ladies in London!" A few murmurs of excitement and interest chased after her announcement. "Please, do come and join me."

"Lord Kensington is not to appear, then," said a voice in his ear, and Jeffery turned to see Lord Swinton chuckling as he moved past Jeffery slowly, a lady on his arm. "How very unsurprising."

"Lady Kensington states that he is in his study," Jeffery replied, joining his friend. "Mayhap I should go to speak with him and—"

"Do not be so foolish!" Lord Swinton exclaimed, suddenly rounding on Jeffery and letting go of the lady on his arm. "You cannot do such a thing, for it is not your duty. Lady Kensington will take his place, just as she has done before, and all will be well."

"It was Lady Kensington herself who suggested I do so," Jeffery replied, only for Lord Swinton to throw up his hands and roll his eyes in apparent frustration.

"You are much too compassionate, old boy," came the firm reply. "Can you not see that she fully intends to make use of your willingness to, perhaps, *force* her attentions on you?" He shook his head and pointed to the door. "That is the only place you ought to go at present. Do not allow your kind heart to be misled."

Jeffery nodded slowly, fully aware that perhaps his heart was a little too sympathetic given the circumstances. He made to follow Lord Swinton through into the adjoining room, only to hesitate. Lady Kensington would not be able to follow him and certainly could have no intention of 'forcing' her attentions upon him given that she would be caught up with the responsibilities of ensuring her guests were comfortable and contented. Was he being much too harsh in his judgment of her?

"And I have not yet even greeted Lord Kensington," Jeffery muttered, still feeling a nudge of guilt over the fact that he had been so very late in the first place. Seeing how Lord Swinton hurried to catch the lady he had been walking with and knowing full well that his friend would be all the more distracted by her, Jeffery took in a deep breath and made his decision.

∼

"Lord Kensington?"

Rapping on the door lightly, Jeffery looked up and down the hallway but saw no staff. Was Lord Kensington within? Or had he gone elsewhere? A flurry of doubt ran through him as he knocked again, telling himself that he needed to return quickly to the drawing-room rather than remain here. Perhaps Lady Kensington had been mistaken. Her husband clearly was not where she believed him to be, and now he felt very foolish indeed for even attempting to do what she had suggested. Lord Swinton had been correct, it seemed. Jeffery's heart was much too compassionate.

Sighing, he turned away and began to retrace his steps back to the drawing-room. He would have to slip back inside quietly so as not to draw attention to himself, but, given that most of the guests would be listening to whichever young lady was either singing or playing the pianoforte, that would not be too difficult.

"Lord Richmond, I knew you would come!"

A breathless voice ripped through the quiet of the hallway, only for a figure to throw itself into Jeffery's arms, startling him completely. In the dim candlelight, he looked down to see none other than Lady Kensington gazing up at him with evident ardor smoldering in her eyes, her hands already around his neck.

"Lady Kensington," Jeffery spluttered, trying to remove himself from her but finding that she was very determined in her attempts to remain close to him. "Whatever are you doing?"

A laugh escaped from the lady's parted lips as Jeffery stumbled back against the wall, taking Lady Kensington with him.

"You surely cannot pretend that you are unaware of my intentions, Lord Richmond," she said, pressing herself against him as he struggled to remove her hands from around his neck, panic beginning to rise in his chest. "And now, here you are, waiting for me!"

Jeffery shook his head, managing, finally, to unclasp the lady's arms from his neck. Without wanting to overpower her, he pushed her back a few steps, his hands still holding her arms so that she could not force herself back against him again.

"I went to see if Lord Kensington was in his study, as you suggested," he said, as firmly as he could. "I had no other intention!"

"I suggested no such thing!" Lady Kensington protested, a teasing note in her voice that sent a shudder down Jeffery's spine. "But what does such a confusion matter now? You have stepped away from the other guests, and I have found myself here with you. This is an opportune moment, Lord Richmond. Can you not see that?"

Jeffery shook his head. "No, Lady Kensington," he replied firmly, releasing her arms carefully and watching her with a keen eye, beginning to edge away from her as though she were a trap that had just been set. "I have no desire to do such a thing. You are very lovely indeed, and I cannot pretend that you are not a diamond of the first water, but—"

"Your words speak to my heart!" Lady Kensington made to throw herself at him again and, having no other course but to catch her for fear that she would then fall to the floor if he did not, Jeffery once more found himself in the same situation he had only just escaped from. Her hands were about his neck, her lips close to his as she lifted her chin, beseeching words escaping her, but no sense of ardor hurried into Jeffery's heart. Instead, he felt repulsed by her, silently cursing his own foolishness as, once more, he fought to escape.

"Who goes there?"

A gasp escaped from Lady Kensington's lips as Jeffery's frame went stiff with fright. Finally managing to push her arms away from him, he cleared his throat abruptly. There was no good pretending that he had not heard the voice, that he was not aware of being seen by another. He could not recognize the voice nor make out the face of the person now standing only a short distance away, their figure nothing more than a dark shadow.

"I am just returning from the study," he said honestly. "It is I, Lord Richmond. I had hoped to find Lord Kensington, but alas, I have been unable to do so."

"That is because I was not in my study," came the reply, and Jeffery's heart sank to the floor. Lord Kensington, it seemed, was the one who had come upon them both. "Lord Millerton and I were in the library. We are returning to the soiree now."

"Then permit me to join you," Jeffery replied, ignoring the fact that Lady Kensington was nearby and silently praying that she would remain wherever she was until they had departed. Walking closer to Lord Kensington, he quickly noticed Lord Millerton standing close by also, his features illuminated by candlelight as he stepped forward. The man's eyes quickly darted away from Jeffery, looking a little embarrassed as he drew near. Did they both suspect that Lady Kensington was present still? He prayed that Lord Kensington would accept his explanation and would return to the drawing-room so that nothing more would be said.

"Lord Richmond." Lord Kensington turned to Jeffery, his eyes a little hooded as he looked up at him. "I presume my wife is here also?"

The question was shocking in itself, and, for a moment, Jeffery did not know what to say. Should he tell the gentleman the truth? That he had been caught unawares by Lady Kensington and that he had been attempting to remove himself from her? Or should he instead pretend that he knew nothing of what Lord Kensington spoke, ignoring the guilt that slammed into his heart at the thought?

"If she is, Lord Kensington, I am unaware of it," he lied, spreading his hands. "I swear to you that my only intention was to return to the drawing-room, having come from your study."

"I was not in my study."

"I am aware of that," Jeffery replied a little desperately. "But I was informed that the room you were in was the study, and thus, in order to both satisfy my own need to greet you, as well as assisting Lady Kensington with her desire to have you present, I thought to make my way there at once."

Lord Kensington studied Jeffery for some moments, leaving him feeling most uncomfortable. His heart began to quicken as Lord Kensington shook his head and sighed, fearful now that his lie and his truths would be for naught. What the gentleman would believe, Jeffery could not say, but whatever came of it, Jeffery knew his reputation was at stake.

"It is true, husband."

He closed his eyes tightly, swaying just a little as the voice of Lady Kensington reached his ears. He had been so very close to achieving what he required, of making certain that the truth was kept from Lord Kensington, and now she had ruined it all.

"Lady Kensington," Lord Kensington said heavily, tearing his eyes away from Jeffery and looking back out towards the dark hallway. "I did expect you to be here, I confess."

"But it is not for the reasons you think," Lady Kensington replied, clearly able to lie just as easily as Jeffery had done. "I was gone in search of the retiring room and simply happened upon Lord Richmond in passing."

Lord Kensington lifted his candle a little higher so that he might look into his wife's beautiful face a little more, and Jeffery was astonished at the open, vulnerable expression that was there now. The lady was lying openly to her husband and yet appeared to be greatly sorrowful, almost overcome with emotion.

"It is not as you suspect, Lord Kensington," she said eagerly as Jeffery shook his head to himself, running one hand over his forehead. "Please, you must not be so suspicious. It was nothing more than an accidental meeting."

Lord Kensington glanced at Jeffery and then looked back to his wife. Jeffery felt as though he were walking along a knife's edge, waiting for judgment to fall upon him. Aware that Lord Millerton was watching this interaction and that, no doubt, the rumors about him would soon spread through all of society, Jeffery closed his eyes and prayed that it would not ruin his reputation. He could not have such a thing occur, not when the Season itself had only just begun!

"My dear little wife," he heard Lord Kensington say, his voice soft with a tenderness Jeffery had not expected. "The wife I believed cared for me in the same way that I cared for her. The wife who has chosen to throw her affections towards any gentleman she chooses. The wife who has become the person I now begin to despise." He shook his head and looked back at Jeffery. "I do not know what to believe, Lord Richmond," he continued, speaking slowly so that every word had the impression of being carefully chosen. "My wife is inclined towards such things and has lied to me so many times before. But you, however, are an upstanding gentleman who, I expect, would be more inclined towards speaking the truth than falsehoods." Pressing his lips together, he considered things a little longer with sweat breaking out on Jeffery's brow. He wanted to speak up, wanted to defend himself a little more but could find nothing to say. Lord Kensington was clearly uncertain as to what to do or what to believe, and Jeffery, for the moment, could only wait.

"I think, Lord Richmond, that I must ask you to leave my house."

Jeffery's mouth fell open. "But I—I have not done—"

"Whether or not you have done anything, I cannot have a gentleman who was alone with my wife for a time continue to linger under my roof." Lord Kensington's voice was hard, his obvious upset now beginning to show. "I will ask you to depart at once, Lord Richmond."

"My dear husband!" Lady Kensington's voice was quietly pleading, her voice soft and her eyes turned towards her husband's. "Lord Richmond has done nothing to deserve your wrath."

"You would both have me believe that, but I, for one, am not at all certain," came the harsh reply. "You have lied to me too many times, Cordelia. Lord Richmond may have a good character, but that does not mean he will not fall where other gentlemen have fallen also." Clearing his throat, he turned his attention back to Jeffery. "If you please, Lord Richmond. I will have your carriage brought immediately. Good evening to you."

Jeffery could find nothing to say. He wanted to protest, wanted to beg Lord Kensington to reconsider for fear that his reputation would be affected by what had occurred this night. But Lord Kensington was already walking away, his wife trailing alongside him and Lord Millerton walking only a few steps behind.

Closing his eyes, Jeffery dragged in a shaky breath, cursing himself and his foolishness. He ought never to have given in to his own compassionate nature. Had he not done so, he would now be sitting with the other guests, listening to some music and singing without a care in all of the world. Now, he found himself thrown from Lord Kensington's house, asked to depart when he had done nothing worthy of such disgrace—but disgrace it was, and it would linger around his neck for some time to come. No doubt Lord Millerton would tell all and sundry of what he had heard, of what he had seen—if not adding a few extra details that would make things all the worse. Jeffery would barely be able to lift his head, such would be his shame!

But there was nothing to be done. The decision had been made. Jeffery now had nothing further to do but to depart from the house knowing that, by the time he awoke in the morning, everything would be very different indeed.

CHAPTER FOUR

Rebecca looked at herself doubtfully in the full-length mirror, whilst Lady Hayward watched closely, admiring the new gown and considering it from every angle.

"What do you think, Lady Rebecca?" the seamstress asked, clearly a little anxious. "Does it fit well?"

"Very well," Rebecca admitted, considering it carefully. "It is only the color that I am a little unsure of."

Lady Hayward smiled but said nothing, leaving Rebecca to continue to look at herself in the lovely gown. It was a very gentle green, which was an unusual color for those who were stepping out in London for the first time. Most young ladies would be in gowns of cream or yellow, but Lady Hayward had stated that yellow, certainly, would do nothing for Rebecca's complexion and would have the effect of making her look a little sickly. Cream, of course, was very acceptable indeed, but the concern was that every other young lady in London would be wearing such colors, and Lady Hayward was eager for Rebecca to stand out.

"I think it is very lovely on you," Lady Anna remarked from where she and Selina sat. "It may be a little different in color from the other gowns we see, but that does not mean that it is at all not pretty or unsuitable."

"No, indeed. I think it suits you very well," Lady Selina added quietly. "But you must have the confidence to believe it, I think."

A little irritated that her younger sisters knew her as well as that, Rebecca let out a heavy sigh and then turned around again, trying to look at the gown from every angle. "Lady Hayward?" she asked, feeling a little hopeless. "What say you?"

Lady Hayward smiled, tilting her head just a fraction. "I think it is as your sister says, Lady Rebecca. It is a very well-suited gown. It fits you perfectly, and it is only the color that might be a little unusual. But if you have the confidence to wear it into society, I can promise that everyone will think you very lovely indeed."

"And that is what we seek, is it not?" Lady Anna chirped, her bright expression one of eagerness and anticipation. "We seek to make an impression upon any particular gentlemen that have caught our notice, and I am certain, Rebecca, that this gown will do that very well indeed."

Despite her misgivings and her lack of confidence, Rebecca forced herself to nod. "Yes, I think you are right," she murmured, stepping back a little more and turning her eyes away from the mirror. "Thank you,

Madame Bernadotte. I shall be very happy with this dress."

The lady looked relieved. "I am very glad to hear it, Lady Rebecca," she answered with a small, quick curtsy. "If you would like to change, then I will have this gown finished by the morrow."

"I thank you," Rebecca replied as she stepped back towards the small room where she might change back into her walking dress. "I will be but a few minutes."

Upon returning, Rebecca found Lady Hayward and Selina deep in discussion over a pair of very fine evening gloves, whilst Anna was looking at some new ribbons that had all been laid out. Forcing a smile to her face and praying that she would not be asked about her true feelings on the gown—feelings of uncertainty and doubt rather than confidence—Rebecca came to join Lady Hayward and her sister.

"Then we are satisfied here for a time?" Lady Hayward said brightly as Rebecca nodded. "What shall we do next, then? There is a wonderful bookshop nearby, and I would be glad to show you all where it is. Or we might take tea somewhere?" She lifted one shoulder. "Or if you are fatigued, then we could have the carriage take you home."

"No, indeed not!" Lady Anna cried, suddenly appearing from behind Rebecca. "I am not at all fatigued. The bookshop and then perhaps somewhere to take tea?" She looked at Rebecca, who merely nodded, not particularly concerned with what they did or where they went.

"The bookshop, then," Lady Hayward smiled. "Come now, it is just this way."

Rebecca fell into step just behind Lady Hayward, making certain to thank the seamstress as she left. Madame Bernadotte seemed very pleased indeed with what had occurred, and that, at least, made Rebecca smile. The seamstress had done a wonderful job, certainly, for the gowns that had been made for her sisters and now also for her, were of the highest quality and could not be faulted in any way.

If only it were not green!

"So, Lady Rebecca," Lady Hayward began as they stepped outside. "You have been in London society for over a sennight now. In fact, almost a fortnight, I believe!" Her eyes twinkled as Rebecca's two sisters linked arms and walked ahead together, leaving Rebecca and Lady Hayward to speak quietly.

"It has been almost a fortnight since we met, yes," Rebecca agreed. "It does not seem as though all that time has passed, however!"

"And yet, it has done so," Lady Hayward replied, her expression one of interest. "You have had time to become acquainted with some gentlemen, to dance with them, converse with them, and the like. Tell me," she continued, "is there any gentleman with whom you are taken?"

Heat climbed into Rebecca's face, and she shook her head.

"None?" Lady Hayward remarked, sounding a little astonished. "My goodness, then I fear I have failed in my duties thus far! I was certain I had introduced you to the most eligible of gentlemen!"

"Pray, do not think so!" Rebecca exclaimed, not wanting to injure Lady Hayward's feelings in any way.

"They have all been very gentlemanly indeed, with some being so good as to call upon me the following afternoon, as you well know, but Lord Arbuckle, for example, talks incessantly of his good fortune at the card table and Lord Winchester speaks very little at all!" She shook her head, a little frustrated with both herself and the gentlemen who had come to greet her. "I find them all a little lacking, Lady Hayward," she finished, now all the more embarrassed that she felt such a way. "I do not mean to undermine your judgment nor your choices in considering these gentlemen, but I must admit to—"

"You speak the truth, and that is all that concerns me at present," Lady Hayward replied with evident determination and not a flicker of upset in her gaze. "I would much prefer the truth from you than a pretense, Lady Rebecca. Surely you must know that by now!"

Rebecca smiled and looked back at the lady. Over the last ten days, she had come to think very highly of Lady Hayward. She was very fair in her judgments, open in her thoughts, and always careful to listen whenever Rebecca had something to say. She had encouraged Rebecca gently, had not pushed her when she felt uncomfortable, and had done all she could to allow Rebecca the freedom to make her own decisions about the gentlemen she had been introduced to. Lady Hayward had not forced her to accept a dance from any gentleman at all, had not eagerly pressed her towards a gentleman she considered to be very suitable indeed. Rather, she had spoken plainly about each one and allowed Rebecca to choose for herself.

"I hope you do not think me foolish in finding such

faults, Lady Hayward," Rebecca said suddenly, fear lurching in her heart. "I know that they are all very eligible indeed and certainly would do very well for me, but there is always something about each one that troubles me."

Lady Hayward laughed and looped her arm through Rebecca's. "No, indeed not, Lady Rebecca!" she exclaimed, a sigh of relief escaping from Rebecca's lips. "I should not think poorly of you for exercising such caution! I have been the one to encourage it within you, have I not?" She smiled and shook her head. "Indeed, I would prefer you to continue to exercise such judgment, Lady Rebecca, for to make a choice in haste is never wise." Her expression softened, her gaze a little distant. "It took me some months before I would even accept the attentions of my late husband when we were first introduced. He tried for the entirety of the Season to capture my interest, but I was not sure of him."

"Oh?" Rebecca murmured, suddenly intrigued by all that Lady Hayward had to say. "But he convinced you in the end?"

Lady Hayward nodded, her smile now a little sorrowful. "My father remained in London over the winter, and thus I found myself often in Lord Hayward's company," she said quietly. "By the time spring had come, I was engaged, and our wedding was set for the month of April. He had thoroughly convinced me of his devotion, his affection, and his eagerness to wed, Lady Rebecca. And even now, so many years later, even when he is gone, I am glad that I chose to consider him for so long before accepting. Therefore, I would expect the same from you."

Rebecca let out a small sigh, turning her head so that she did not have to look at Lady Hayward any longer. There was something both very beautiful and yet very sad about her story, and Rebecca's heart was already beginning to ache. "I do not think that my father would be best pleased if I did not find a suitable match this Season, Lady Hayward," she replied heavily. "I do not think that I have the same luxury of time as you."

A smile crept across Lady Hayward's face. "I am sure that your father could be convinced otherwise, Lady Rebecca," she said encouragingly. "Do not permit any such fears to hurry you into an engagement."

Rebecca nodded but said nothing more, with Lady Hayward dropping her hand from Rebecca's arm so that she might catch Lady Selina and Lady Anna who were now standing close to the bookshop they intended to enter, waiting for their chaperone to enter first. Rebecca sighed softly to herself, trying not to allow any sort of panic to grasp a hold of her heart. It was very difficult, indeed, trying to allow her thoughts to remain calm and controlled when it came to her considerations for matrimony and the like.

On the one hand, she had Lady Hayward, who was encouraging her to take her time, to consider carefully and to think not only of what her father would like in a suitable match for her, but also what *she* would prefer in a husband. On the other, she had the Duke, who was more than eager for his eldest daughter to wed, regardless of what Rebecca herself wanted. So long as *his* requirements were met, then the gentleman would be considered suitable. Would Lady Hayward be able to convince him that good matches took time? Would she be able to encourage him to allow Rebecca another Season, if she did not find a suitable gentleman this year?

You are letting your thoughts take hold of you, Rebecca, she told herself firmly. *Do not worry so.*

It had been a very different way of thinking, of course, for Rebecca had never truly considered what she really wanted when it came to a husband. She had only ever thought of what would be agreeable to her father, rather than to herself. But now, Rebecca was beginning to consider what *she* would like—and that was both surprising and intriguing to her. She discovered that she did not like overly loud gentlemen, who were bold and brash and laughed a good deal. She certainly did not like the way some of them looked at her, eyeing her as though she were some sort of prize that they might be able to claim as their own. No, she thought to herself, hurrying towards the open bookshop door so that she might step inside after her sisters, she much preferred a gentleman who was a little quieter in his character, who did not try to catch the attention of others with his overt remarks or his brash laughter. Rather, she enjoyed the company of those who spoke with consideration and tact, who did not look at her as though she were nothing of consequence save for how she might look on their arm.

The bookshop was quiet as Rebecca stepped inside, immediately filling her with a sense of peace. Lady Hayward was speaking quietly with her sisters, who then nodded and separated, each perusing the shelves quickly and silently. Rebecca, a little surprised that they seemed so eager to purchase a book when they had not ever shown much interest in reading, merely shrugged her shoulders and made her way to another part of the bookshop, her fingers lingering on one or two of the books as she meandered slowly towards the back of the shop.

Rounding the end of one of the shelves, Rebecca caught herself just in time, seeing a gentleman standing just before her, his head bowed as he looked through a page of the book he held in his hand. Obviously, he had not yet seen her, for his countenance did not change and he did not even look up—but he stood directly in Rebecca's path and blocked her way entirely.

She cleared her throat gently, a little embarrassed to have to do so, and the gentleman lifted his eyes from the book immediately.

"Forgive me!" he exclaimed, stepping aside at once. "I did not mean to block your path."

Rebecca looked into a pair of blue eyes and found herself smiling, touched by the gentleman's immediate apology. "It is quite all right," she replied, keeping her voice low so as not to disturb the quietness of the shop. "You must be very interested in whatever book you are reading." She lifted one eyebrow, expressing quiet curiosity whilst knowing full well that they had not been properly introduced and that, as such, she ought to continue on without remaining to converse further.

But there was something about him that made her want to linger, even though she could not quite place what it was. Perhaps it was the look of embarrassment that was now etched across his face, his cheeks warm and his eyes darting from one place to the next, or perhaps it was simply that she *was*, in fact, a little interested to know what it was that had caught his attention with such fervor.

"It is...a novel," he replied, clearly still a little embarrassed. "Nothing of particular interest, but I found myself drawn in." He cleared his throat and set the book down. "It is not the sort of book I usually engage with, but on this occasion..." He shrugged, and then, his gaze shifting to something over Rebecca's shoulder, cleared his throat abruptly and inclined his head. "Good afternoon, Lady Hayward."

Rebecca turned at once, surprised at the expression on Lady Hayward's face. She was not smiling but was looking at the gentleman with sharp eyes, her lips thin and her brows furrowed.

"Good afternoon, Lord Richmond," she said, a coldness in her voice that Rebecca had not heard before. "I see that you are acquainting yourself with my charge."

Lord Richmond's face lost all color as he looked back at Lady Hayward, making Rebecca wonder what had been implied by such a remark. Looking from one to the next, she was forced to make a small murmur towards Lady Hayward, clearly requesting an introduction that, as yet, had not been made.

Lady Hayward did not look pleased.

"Might I present Lady Rebecca, daughter to the Duke of Landon," she said tightly. "Lady Rebecca, this is the Marquess of Richmond."

A little surprised at Lady Hayward's fierce reaction to a gentleman that was of such a good title, Rebecca curtsied quickly and hoped that her astonishment did not show in her expression. "How very good to meet you,

Lord Richmond," she said, as he bowed formally towards her. "You are in town for the Season, then?"

"I am," Lord Richmond replied as Lady Hayward took a small step closer to Rebecca as though attempting to stand directly between her and Lord Richmond. Rebecca did not understand what was occurring and thus merely looked at Lady Hayward for a long moment, only for the lady to turn her gaze back towards Lord Richmond.

"You intend to remain in London, then?" Lady Hayward asked, her voice still tight, her words clipped. "You will stay for the rest of the Season?"

Lord Richmond drew himself up. His shoulders rose, his chin lifted, and he gazed back at Lady Hayward with something akin to frustration flickering in his eyes.

"I will remain in London, Lady Hayward, for there is no reason for me to depart," he said, coolly. "You may wish to believe the rumors, but I will stand before you now and state unequivocally that I am innocent of any wrongdoing."

Rebecca shifted uncomfortably, aware of the tension that was now growing between both Lord Richmond and Lady Hayward. She had no knowledge as to what they spoke of, but it was clear that Lady Hayward's apparent dislike of Lord Richmond came from something he had evidently done. Something that he, it seemed, was now vehemently denying.

"You will hardly wish to believe me, of course," Lord Richmond continued, "but surely you know, Lady Hayward, that rumors and gossip can often come from something that is entirely different from what is being spoken of. Whispers grow into all manner of stories until the person involved in such a tale has no other choice but to hide away from society until it passes from the *beau monde*'s sphere. And that might well take many months, if not years, in some cases. Therefore, I have decided I shall *not* return to my estate, for in doing so, I believe that I would make it quite plain that I have something to hide from, that there is some truth in these rumors. Therefore, I am not doing so. I shall remain here without fear and without reservation."

Lady Hayward did not reply for some moments. She considered Lord Richmond, looking at him steadily, although her expression did not change. Rebecca said nothing, wondering what it was that Lord Richmond had apparently done yet knowing that she could not ask outright.

"Regardless of whether or not you are innocent or guilty of such rumors, Lord Richmond, you must be aware that you cannot linger by the side of a lady such as this," Lady Hayward remarked, gesturing to Rebecca. "A daughter of a duke, who is in London for the very first time?" She shook her head at him, clearly all the more displeased. "You may consider yourself innocent, Lord Richmond, but the *ton* does not, and they will taint whomever it is that you keep in your company. Therefore, you will excuse us both."

Lord Richmond opened his mouth to protest and then, after a moment, closed it again. A long sigh issued from his mouth as he shook his head and ran long fingers through his thick, dark hair. Rebecca watched him carefully and, to her surprise, felt a rush of sympathy in her heart for the man. She did not know this gentleman at all, had barely said more than a few words to him, and yet, from his appearance alone, she found herself filled with compassion. If he was being tossed about by the *ton* and their malicious rumors, then she could not help but feel for him and his present circumstance. Studying him carefully, she took in the dark smudges underneath his eyes, the way his mouth tugged downwards. Lines formed across his forehead as he frowned, his jaw working furiously for a few moments as he slowly lifted his gaze back towards Lady Hayward.

"Good afternoon, Lady Hayward," he muttered before turning back to Rebecca. "Good afternoon, Lady Rebecca. It was my honor to be introduced to you."

"And I to you," Rebecca found herself saying, ignoring the sharp look from Lady Hayward. Lord Richmond said nothing more, turning on his heel and making his way to another part of the bookshop, leaving the novel he had been so engaged in sitting quietly on the shelf.

Lady Hayward let out a long breath of relief.

"I am sorry for the abruptness of my manner, Lady Rebecca, but you cannot associate yourself with such a gentleman," she said firmly, astonishing Rebecca greatly. "I am doing it for your own good, for Lord Richmond is not a gentleman that you ought to converse with." She turned to face Rebecca a little more, her gaze severe. "He may be a marquess, but there is a rumor about him that has flown through the *ton* with such force that I do not think he will be able to remove it from his person for even the following Season!" With a small sigh, she reached to catch Rebecca's hand, her eyes searching Rebecca's face. "You do quite understand, I hope?"

Rebecca hesitated, looking back at Lady Hayward and choosing to speak the truth rather than merely agreeing without discussion. "Might I ask, Lady Hayward, what it is that he has done? Why is it that I must not be in his company, particularly if he is denying what has occurred?"

"Because," Lady Hayward said with a sigh, spreading her hands, "the *ton* do not see it that way. I confess to not giving his words even a momentary consideration. Many times has a gentleman claimed not to be guilty of what is being said of him, only for it to soon be revealed that he has done precisely what is being whispered, if not more. Either way, it is best for you to remain away from him, Lady Rebecca. It is not wise for you to be in his company."

Rather than accepting this, Rebecca found something small beginning to burrow into her heart. An urge to rebel and tell Lady Hayward that she did not want to do such a thing and did not have any intention of doing so. It was remarkably strange to have such a reaction for, whilst she did not know Lady Hayward particularly well, Rebecca already trusted her guidance and advice. So why should she step back from it now?

"What do the rumors say?" she asked, pressing Lady Hayward again for the answer. "If I am to remain away from him, then I must know the truth."

Lady Hayward frowned. "Why should it matter, Lady Rebecca?" she asked, clearly unwilling to speak of whatever it was that had evidently occurred. "You were only briefly introduced to him and have no need to return to his company."

There was no simple way to express her strange desire to know more, to tell Lady Hayward the reason for her eagerness. Given that she could not express it herself, Rebecca could only shrug and look away. "Call it curiosity," she replied, a little embarrassed. "It is not something I can easily express but there is an urge within me to know what is being said of him." Her lips twisted for a moment as she struggled to find a way to state clearly what was within her heart and mind. "He seemed very determined to state his innocence, Lady Hayward. And to remain in London when he is clearly considered guilty must take great strength of character and surely must speak of his lack of guilt?"

Lady Hayward sighed and closed her eyes, opening them after only a moment. "You are interested in Lord Richmond, then. Quite what he has said to you to make you so eager for his company, I cannot imagine, for you were only together for a few minutes before I came to join you!"

"I am not interested in him in that sense," Rebecca protested weakly. "But rather to know what it is that has caused such consternation." Warming to the explanation she now clung to, she shrugged one shoulder. "I have never seen you behave in such a way towards a gentleman before, Lady Hayward. You can hardly expect me not to seek out the truth of this rumor given that it has practically pushed me from his company!"

This did not appear to convince Lady Hayward, who shook her head, ran one hand across her brows as she muttered something inaudible that Rebecca took to be nothing more than frustration. A knot of anxiety sat in her stomach as she waited for Lady Hayward to say more, wanting desperately to know now the truth of the matter.

"It is to do with a lady named Lady Kensington," Lady Hayward said eventually, lifting her head. "She is, from what I understand, something of a...flirt."

"I see," Rebecca replied slowly. "And she is wed, I presume?"

"Yes, she is not a widow or any such thing," Lady Hayward replied with a grimace. "She is wed to the Earl of Kensington, who is a very respected gentleman, although he is certainly a good deal older than his wife."

This did not surprise Rebecca in any way, for she had been told that such things often occurred. A gentleman who had not married earlier in life would seek out a younger wife in order to produce both the heir and the required spare. Evidently, this was the case with Lord and Lady Kensington.

"However, given that Lady Kensington is known to behave so, it is wise for respectable gentlemen of the *ton* to remain out of her company should they wish to maintain their reputations. It appears that Lord Richmond was not doing so."

A small frown crossed Rebecca's forehead. "He was in her company, then?"

"When her husband—and everyone else, it seems—was absent," Lady Hayward replied delicately. "It is not known the precise details, I will say, but the rumors have been flying around London for a few days now. It seems that Lord Richmond and Lady Kensington were discovered by her husband in a less-than-proper situation. Lord Richmond denies such a thing whilst Lady Kensington has said nothing and now remains steadfastly by her husband's side." She looked at Rebecca steadily. "Does that now satisfy your curiosity?"

There was no immediate response from Rebecca, who considered all that Lady Hayward had said without instant judgment. Lord Richmond had been quite determined to state his innocence, had been eager to impress upon them both that he had not done anything that the rumors suggested, and yet Lady Hayward was determined to take her from his company without any hesitation. That was, of course, very wise indeed, but there was still something within Rebecca that felt the unfairness of it all. She wanted to know whether or not Lord Richmond spoke the truth, for if he did, then was there any particular reason she could not be in his company?

Why are you so eager to see him again? came a quiet voice in her head. *It is not at all sensible. You ought to be accepting of what Lady Hayward had said and, in doing so, remove yourself from his company. Why do you seek out more?*

"Lady Rebecca?"

Taking in a deep breath, Rebecca gave Lady Hayward a tight smile, one that she had to force to her lips. "I understand why you wish me to remain far from him," she said honestly. "However, I struggle to accept that a gentleman who states clearly that he has done no wrong should be so rejected by society, and by myself also."

Lady Hayward's brows lifted, and she spread her

hands. "What else would you wish to do, Lady Rebecca?" she asked, as Rebecca frowned. "Continue to seek him out? To improve your acquaintance with him when the very act of doing such a thing might only damage your own, perfect reputation?" She waited for Rebecca to respond and, aware of the truth of what was said, Rebecca could only sigh, nod, and look away.

"I do not know what it is about Lord Richmond that has caught your attention so, but I can assure you that there will be plenty of other gentlemen who are eager to make your acquaintance," Lady Hayward finished, putting a hand on Rebecca's arm. "Come now, let us go in search of your sisters. And perhaps you might like to find something to purchase also?"

On instinct, Rebecca reached for the book that Lord Richmond had put down, picking it up and studying it for a moment. "Yes," she said slowly, knowing that Lady Hayward would have no knowledge of why she had chosen this particular book and yet feeling a small stab of guilt in doing so. "I should like to purchase this one, I think. And perhaps another also."

"You enjoy reading?"

Lady Hayward was smiling now, clearly glad that their discussion about Lord Richmond was at an end.

"I do," Rebecca replied honestly. "My sisters are not at all inclined to do so, however, so I shall be very surprised indeed if they have found anything of interest!"

This made Lady Hayward laugh, and the remaining tension that had lingered ever since Lord Richmond had left their company quickly dissipated.

"Then let us go and see what they have discovered,"

Lady Hayward said as Rebecca nodded and followed after her. "And I thank you for your understanding, Lady Rebecca. Society can be a very difficult thing to traverse, and you are doing very well thus far. I should not like you to injure yourself in any way."

"You are doing your very best to protect and guide me, and for that, I am truly appreciative," Rebecca replied, trying not to look down at the book in her hand as a fresh wave of guilt thrust itself, hard at her soul. "It must be very difficult for Lord Richmond, but I ought not to think of *his* difficulties at present but look entirely to my own situation."

Lady Hayward glanced over her shoulder, a small smile on her face. "That is it precisely, Lady Rebecca," she stated, clearly satisfied. "And tonight's ball will be another opportunity for you to further your own situation. I am sure that, by this evening, you will have forgotten about Lord Richmond entirely."

Rebecca said nothing and waited as Lady Hayward went to speak to her sisters. Despite her awareness of the situation, despite her knowledge that she ought not to be thinking of the gentleman any longer, the way he had spoken to Lady Hayward and the way he had drawn himself up in defense, would not leave her mind. Whilst Lady Hayward might be quite certain that Rebecca would be able to forget him, Rebecca herself did not think it would be as simple as she expected. Lord Richmond had captured her attention in a single moment and, for whatever reason, Rebecca found she did not want to remove him from her thoughts, even if it might be the best thing for her.

CHAPTER FIVE

"Are you certain you should be here?"

Jeffery drew himself up, looking hard at Lord Swinton as he prepared to make his defense, but his friend quickly held up both hands in a defensive gesture.

"What I mean to say is, whilst you have been invited and whilst you are, of course, welcome to attend, do you believe that it is in your best interest to be here?" He studied Jeffery carefully. "The rumors have only just begun."

"I am aware of that," Jeffery replied tightly. "But I am determined to prove to the *ton* that I am not about to hide away as though I am guilty."

Lord Swinton drew in a breath and then shrugged. "I suppose that is one way to go about things," he replied, a trifle begrudgingly. "However, what if you are thoroughly rejected by the *ton*? That will not make for a pleasant Season."

"It is better than hiding away, knowing that such rumors are being whispered," Jeffery remarked, hiding the true extent of his frustration from his friend. "There is no truth in what they say of me. I am not the sort of gentleman to steal another man's wife!"

An expression of sympathy appeared on Lord Swinton's face. "I am aware of that," he replied, a little more kindly. "As are, I am sure, many within the *beau monde*. But not everyone will accept such a thing. I am, of course, attempting to defend you as much as I can, but the truth of the matter is that there are those within the *beau monde* who like nothing more than to chew over some piece of gossip and disregard entirely the notion that it might, in some way, affect a gentleman's character. The rumor mill is more important to them than anything else."

Jeffery sighed inwardly and shrugged as though such a thing was of no great consequence. "Let them say what they wish," he stated as firmly as he could despite the fact that he felt no such confidence within his heart. "I am determined to prove myself to the *ton* in one way or another. I shall not allow myself to be treated as though I have done something wrong when I have not."

Lord Swinton spread his hands. "You are welcome to try although I think it will be most difficult," he said with a shake of his head. "Although, might I ask something?"

Jeffery nodded. "But of course."

"What precisely occurred that evening?" Lord Swinton asked slowly. "I simply recall that you did not return to the soiree and when Lady Kensington finally reappeared—for she had begged us all to excuse her for a few minutes—it was more than apparent that she had been crying. Lord Kensington took unwell and did not even come and greet his guests, and when Lord Millerton returned, he said nothing but encouraged the gentlemen to join him at Whites."

"Where, no doubt, the rumors began," Jeffery muttered, darkly. "What did he say, exactly?" That evening was still very much in his mind as he recalled the shame of having to return home without being permitted to re-join the other guests. The sleepless night that had followed as he considered all that would happen next, knowing that his reputation would, most likely, be tarnished, and fearful of what would occur thereafter.

"Lord Millerton *was* gleeful," Lord Swinton admitted, a little sadly. "I, of course, did not believe what he said in the least and stated as much, which is, I hope, why there are conflicting accounts of your actions."

Jeffery lifted one eyebrow. "There are?"

"Indeed," Lord Swinton replied, emphatically. "Some say—as Lord Millerton stated—that you were discovered in a most compromising position with Lady Kensington and that, thereafter, you were thrown from the house. Some say that you were merely in conversation with the lady but that you ought not to have been doing such a thing given that she was alone, thereby implying that, had you not been discovered, you would have...*furthered* your acquaintance with her."

A wave of embarrassment flung itself into Jeffery's face. "I see," he muttered, running one hand over his eyes. "And there are none who consider the fact that it might have been Lady Kensington who attempted to capture *my* attention, but *I* was doing all I could to remove myself from her!"

"Is that what happened?" Lord Swinton asked

quietly as the other guests continued to laugh and converse and dance around them. "You were unable to convince her to leave you?"

Another heavy sigh ripped from Jeffery's lips. "I was foolish," he said heavily, hating that he had to admit such a thing aloud but refuse to turn from the truth of it. "I went in search of Lord Kensington, believing him to be in his study." Seeing the widening of Lord Swinton's eyes, Jeffery winced and shook his head. "You told me not to do so, but I did not listen. Upon finding him absent, I decided to return to the soiree. Unfortunately, as I made my way back to the drawing-room, Lady Kensington discovered me in the hallway and attempted to..." Trailing off, he struggled to find the right words. "Attempted to encourage some sort of ardor from me. She did not succeed, however, for I wanted nothing more than to extricate myself from her." Closing his eyes, a small groan escaped him. "You need not tell me that I was unwise. You stated very clearly that my compassion was overruling sense, and you were quite correct. I am certain now that the lady hoped I would do as she asked, in the hope that she might then fling herself at me in the improper fashion that she did. The arrival of her husband and Lord Millerton was, however, quite unexpected."

"You would have escaped without consequence had he not appeared," Lord Swinton added as Jeffery nodded fervently. "And no, I shall not berate you. I believe you have done enough of that on your own."

His shoulders slumping, Jeffery ran one hand through his hair, dislodging the neat style. "Perhaps I should not have come here," he said, suddenly discouraged. "I saw Lady Hayward and met her new charge earlier this afternoon." The pain of what had occurred still bit at him. "She was most unwilling to allow the acquaintance to continue. She practically shunned me and would not listen to my defense!"

"And for that, I am sorry."

Jeffery swung around, astonished to see none other than the young lady he had spoken to in the bookshop standing there, entirely alone. Warnings rose in his head, and he took a small step back. The alarm must have shown on his face, for the lady quickly gestured to an older gentleman who was deep in conversation with another.

"My father, the Duke of Landon," she said, hastily. "I apologize for his distraction."

Jeffery blinked rapidly, not quite certain what to say. Looking to Lord Swinton, he saw the man's eyebrows lift in evident expectation and hastily realized he had not made any sort of introduction.

"Good evening, Lady Rebecca," he said, stumbling over his words such was his surprise. "My dear friend, the Earl of Swinton."

"Good evening, Lord Swinton," came the reply as the young lady curtsied. "I am very glad to make your acquaintance."

"And I yours," Lord Swinton replied, shooting a glance back towards Jeffery. "If you will excuse my ignorance, Lady Rebecca, Lord Richmond has only just informed me that you are in the care of Lady Hayward, and yet—"

"And yet my father is here this evening," Lady

Rebecca interrupted, a smile catching her mouth. "Yes, it is a rather different arrangement, I must say, but my father has many daughters and, without a mother to guide us, he feels the burden of responsibility very heavily indeed. Therefore, Lady Hayward has stepped into the role, although my father does, of course, remain in London and will attend certain social occasions."

Jeffery swallowed hard. He had met this young lady for the first time this afternoon, but she was so markedly different this evening that he could barely lift his eyes from her. Her red curls were tumbling over her shoulders, her green eyes seeming to be all the more vivid as they watched him, her expression a little confused, as though she could not quite understand what he was thinking in watching her so.

"I—I would not like to bring any disgrace to you, Lady Rebecca," Jeffery began, glancing around him and realizing that many of the *ton* would be able to see her talking with him. "To be in my company at present is not recommended."

Lady Rebecca nodded. "I am well aware of that, Lord Richmond," she said practically. "Which is why I shall not linger. I wished only to say that I am sorry for the conversation this afternoon. I believe Lady Hayward is open to the idea that you might not be as guilty as is being spoken of but she is required to protect me from all manner of difficulties."

"I quite understand, Lady Rebecca," Jeffery replied, inclining his head and finding himself surprised at her seemingly genuine consideration of his feelings about the matter. "There is no need to explain. It is very kind of you to think of me so, but I can assure you that Lady Hayward's reaction towards me is the first of many."

This did not seem to please Lady Rebecca, for she bit her lip and frowned, her eyes now fixing to his with an intensity that shook Jeffery's soul. He had no desire to damage this young lady's reputation in any way, and her presence here beside him, her seeming eagerness to discuss the matter with him, was only making things a little more difficult. She ought to be extricating herself from the conversation as quickly as she could before returning to her father's side, and yet, for whatever reason, she was not doing so.

"I do not think it fair, Lord Richmond."

"Fair?" He shot a quick look towards Lord Swinton, who was watching Lady Rebecca with obvious interest, one hand rubbing his chin as Lady Rebecca continued to speak.

"If you are innocent of such a thing, then surely there must be a way to prove it to the *ton*."

Jeffery was stunned. Every other young lady, every other mother or aunt or chaperone would be pulling their charge away from him, telling them that Lord Richmond was not to be trusted, that he was nothing more than a rogue, a scoundrel, and a blaggard, whereas Lady Rebecca, the daughter of a Duke, seemed to believe him to be entirely innocent. It was both refreshing to hear and astonishing to consider, although a warning began to ring as he inclined his head towards her. There was an urge to speak to her further, to agree with her that yes, it was unfair and to express his willingness to try to find a solution to prove his innocence to all and sundry, but in doing so, Jeffery knew that he would be prolonging her time with him, which would, no doubt, soon attract the attention of others.

He had to bring this conversation to a swift end, for her sake.

"I will confess myself quite delighted with the fact that you believe me to be stating the truth when I say that I am not at all what the *ton* considers me to be, Lady Rebecca," he said swiftly, "but there is, I am afraid, nothing that can be done. I must endure, that is all. I must show the *beau monde* that I am unafraid of their hard words, of their whispers and their rumors. Instead, I shall remain here with my head held high in the hope that, one day soon, the gossip will begin to fade away." Shrugging, he gave her a wry smile. "That is all I can hope for, Lady Rebecca, although I thank you for your concern. It is very refreshing in the midst of my difficulties."

She smiled, and Jeffery felt his heart squeeze gently as though he had found something that he wanted desperately to pursue but was being denied from doing so. Looking away from her, he cleared his throat and turned to Lord Swinton. "I believe I should excuse myself, Lord Swinton," he said as his friend lifted one eyebrow. "It would be best, I think. If you could remain to ensure that Lady Rebecca is not—"

"Pray, do not trouble yourself, Lord Richmond." Lady Rebecca's voice was calm and clear, but when he turned to look at her, there was a glint of steel in her eye —although whether or not it was directed towards him for his eagerness to end their conversation, Jeffery could not say.

"I do not wish to trouble you further," Lady Rebecca continued, "and I can see that you also are eager to protect my reputation, which, I suppose, I should be grateful for."

Jeffery frowned, a question on the tip of his tongue as to why she might be displeased about his desire rather than being glad of it, but he restrained himself with effort. Now was not the time to continue speaking to the lady. Not when he was attempting to remove himself from her.

"I do hope we might speak again, Lord Richmond," Lady Rebecca continued, her words astonishing him all the more. "Whilst the *ton* might believe you to be guilty of this particular crime, I find myself believing that you are not as they say."

"You do not even know me, Lady Rebecca," Jeffery stated, unable to keep silent. "How can you make such a judgment?"

Lady Rebecca considered for some moments, tilting her head just a little as she studied him. Jeffery swallowed hard, instantly regretting his question given just how intensely she was now studying him. There was something about her gaze that both unsettled and interested him, as if he were desperate to know what she thought and yet less than willing to ask.

"I do not know what it is, Lord Richmond," came the quiet reply. "But there is something about you that speaks of guiltlessness." One shoulder lifted. "But then again, mayhap I am entirely naïve and will be proven so."

"You are not naïve," Jeffery rumbled, a little overwhelmed by her words. "But all the same, Lady Rebecca, for your own sake—"

"Yes, yes," she said, waving a hand. "Good evening, Lord Richmond. Lord Swinton."

Lord Swinton inclined his head. "Good evening," he murmured as she took her leave, turning back towards her father without a momentary glance back towards Jeffery. Shaking his head, Jeffery looked back at his friend, who was still watching after Lady Rebecca with a slightly astonished look on his face as though he could not believe what he had heard.

"If you were not in such a circumstance, Richmond, I would tell you to pursue that young lady with everything you possessed," he remarked, turning his head to look at Jeffery. "She is quite remarkable!"

"Or very naïve, as she herself stated," Jeffery replied, trying to push away the lingering memory of her watchful eyes considering him and only now becoming aware of just how quickly his heart was beating. "I might be a rogue for all she knows. And given it is her first Season..." He trailed off, leaving the rest of the words unspoken. A debutante did not know much of society, even though she would be well aware of all that was demanded of her in terms of behavior and expectations of propriety. It might come as something of a shock to a delicate young lady to know that gentlemen could be so roguish in their behavior, to hear such whispers and gossip as never before. Quite what it was Lady Rebecca had seen in him, he did not know, but Jeffery was determined to push her from his mind. His only intention was to remain in London and within society to prove to the *ton* that he would not be pushed away by rumor and gossip. Being fully aware that his reputation was already damaged by what had occurred thus far, Jeffery did not want to make it all the worse for himself by running to hide—but he certainly could not pull someone such as Lady Rebecca down with him, even if she *was* both beautiful and intriguing.

"You are in something of a predicament, are you not?" Lord Swinton remarked, shaking his head. "I can tell that you are interested in the lady and, in truth, I do not think I have ever met someone akin to her before. To come here and speak to you in such an open and direct manner, when she has only been introduced to you the once, is quite astonishing!"

"Perhaps she felt a little guilty over what Lady Hayward said to me," Jeffery replied, trying to shrug off any suggestion that he was fascinated by Lady Rebecca. "Although she need not do so. It is not as though it was her doing, and, if I am honest, I quite understand Lady Hayward's need to keep her charge from me, and it is to be expected that gossip such as this is listened to."

Lord Swinton lifted his eyebrows and looked hard at Jeffery, who immediately cleared his throat and looked away. He knew very well that his friend expected him to admit to the fact that he *was* interested in Lady Rebecca when he was quite determined not to do so.

"So, you are to do nothing about the lady, then," Lord Swinton said, sounding disappointed. "You are just to continue as you are, removing her from your thoughts so that you could not even consider her."

"What else is there for me to do?" Jeffery exclaimed,

now becoming a little irritated. "I will admit that she is certainly unusual and that I cannot help but be both flattered and pleased at her remarks, but she is the daughter of a duke! And a debutante at that! If I return to her company, if she is often seen in mine, then her reputation will be tainted! And I will not allow my selfishness to have such an effect."

"Even if you should like to speak to her again?" Lord Swinton asked gently. "Even if she is the only young lady who might be willing to consider you?"

Jeffery blew out a frustrated breath. "Consider me?" he repeated, aware of the mocking tone in his voice but doing nothing to hide it. "I am not even thinking of matrimony, Swinton, as you well know. I certainly could not choose a young lady merely because she might be the only one who would be willing to *consider* marriage!"

Lord Swinton shrugged. "Why not? It is not as though this rumor is going to fade easily. The curse of 'rogue' will follow you for many Seasons. Even when you believe it to be gone, it will still be whispered after you. Ladies will look at you with suspicion; mothers will hold their daughters back from you; worst of all, you may find that the less-than-exemplary ladies seek you out a little more."

It all sounded very dire indeed, and Jeffery shook his head, passing one hand over his eyes as he blew out a long, heavy breath. As much as he wanted to state that there was no truth in anything that Lord Swinton had said, that he did not think there was anything for him to concern himself with for the following Season, Jeffery knew that all he had said was quite true.

"I cannot think of it now," he said, looking around for a footman so that he might find himself something to drink. "Besides which, I am sure that she will not return to converse again with me any time soon. Her chaperone *and* her father will not permit it!"

"We will see," Lord Swinton replied with a gleam in his eye, but Jeffery merely shrugged and took a glass of brandy from the footman's tray. As far as he was concerned, there was nothing further to explore between himself and Lady Rebecca, and in that, he was quite determined.

CHAPTER SIX

Rebecca bobbed a quick curtsy and watched Lord Bellingham as he stepped away. The conversation had been very strained and, whilst Lord Bellingham was very eligible, indeed, there was not even a flicker of interest within her. Nor did she think Lord Bellingham had any desire to continue their acquaintance, given he had appeared to want to end their conversation as quickly as possible.

She sighed inwardly. It had been a sennight since she had last spoken to Lord Richmond, and yet, for whatever reason, she could not remove him from her thoughts. The book she had purchased, the novel that she knew he had been interested in, was still sitting quietly by her bed, whispering to her about him. She had heard some of the gossips herself by now, of course, and had also heard quite a bit about Lady Kensington's reputation and behavior as well. Still, there had been that strong memory of how Lord Richmond had defended himself to Lady Hayward that day in the bookshop.

She wanted to believe him.

"Well?" Lady Hayward's eyes were bright with curiosity, her voice filled with hope. "Did all go well?"

Rebecca let out a quiet sigh and shook her head. "Not as well as you might have expected, Lady Hayward," she said honestly. "Lord Bellingham was difficult to converse with. Unfortunately, he had very little to say."

Lady Hayward's smile dropped from her face in an instant, her brows furrowing a little as she studied Rebecca carefully. "You are saying there was nothing at all of interest?"

"None whatsoever, I'm afraid," Rebecca said, spreading her hands as a slight wave of guilt washed over her. "I wish I could be a little more optimistic, but I fear I cannot."

"It is not your fault," Lady Hayward replied with a sigh. "I thought Lord Bellingham might be all that you required, but if there is no interest there, then I should be loath to encourage you." She smiled briefly, and Rebecca smiled back, relieved that Lady Hayward was not about to force her back into another conversation with Lord Bellingham. "After all, was I not the one to state that there should be, at the very least, a small affection between you and your future husband?" One shoulder lifted in a half shrug. "However, if there is not even a modicum of curiosity in continuing an acquaintance with Lord Bellingham, then we shall not consider him anymore."

"I thank you," Rebecca replied with an inner sigh of relief. "I think, however, you will have to excuse me for a moment. I must seek the retiring room."

Lady Hayward nodded. "But of course." Her eyes began to twinkle in the familiar way that Rebecca had come to know so well. "Mayhap when you return, I will have another gentleman for you to consider!"

Rebecca laughed and made her way from the large drawing room, both relieved and a little nervous about which gentleman Lady Hayward would have next.

∽

"Excuse me," Rebecca murmured, walking past a young lady and making her way slowly back towards the drawing-room. The soiree had, thus far, been quite pleasant, but, as yet, Rebecca had found nothing of particular interest.

"Lord Richmond, please!"

Rebecca froze, her heart beginning to pound immediately as she heard a voice echoing from a little further down the hallway.

"I should not have come."

Knowing that she should not continue to eavesdrop, Rebecca found it entirely impossible to return to the drawing-room. Evidently, Lord Richmond was present and, for whatever reason, was now conversing with another.

"There is no need to behave so. Not with someone such as me."

Rebecca looked over her shoulder, checking that no one else was present in the hallway and watching her. Seeing no one, she quietly made her way forward, nearing the front of Lord and Lady Messick's townhouse.

And Lord Richmond suddenly came into view. He was pushing one hand through his hair, staring hard at the floor whilst a lady stood before him, looking up at him with great earnestness. Rebecca stayed in the shadows, watching closely even though she knew she ought not to be doing so. Her eyes narrowed as she watched the lady, quickly realizing that it was their hostess, Lady Messick, who spoke to him. Her heart turned over in her chest. Had she been mistaken in her first impression of him? Was he now about to prove to her that he was precisely the gentleman society thought him, treating Lady Merrick as he had done Lady Kensington?

"You have friends within society, Lord Richmond," Lady Merrick said urgently and with such eagerness that Rebecca did not know what to think. Was the lady about to press her attentions to Lord Richmond? And was Lord Richmond about to accept?

"I have tried to remain in society," she heard Lord Richmond say, his voice filled with such emotion that Rebecca's stomach twisted. "I have tried these last few days and yet I am met with such vitriol that I have no desire to remain any longer. I...I..." Again, he rubbed one hand over his eye. "I do not think I should have attended this evening, even though I am more than grateful for your consideration in inviting me."

Lady Merrick stepped closer and put one hand on Lord Richmond's arm. Rebecca squeezed her eyes closed, swallowing hard as a twist of fear began to make its way up her spine.

"You are a dear friend to both me and to my husband," she heard Lady Merrick say, the fear beginning to leave her as she opened her eyes to see Lady Merrick stepping back from Lord Richmond. "He is expecting you. We invited you because we do not believe what has been said. We are both very well aware of Lady Kensington's reputation."

Letting out a long, slow breath, Rebecca felt her heart begin to quieten its frantic pace. Lord Richmond was not, as she had feared, about to behave inappropriately with Lady Merrick. A wave of shame crashed over her soul as she turned away, no longer wishing to remain to eavesdrop. Perhaps she should never have done so in the first place.

Turning slowly, Rebecca made her way back to the drawing-room, walking back inside as though nothing had ever occurred. Lady Hayward was waiting for her, gesturing for her to join her again, but Rebecca felt nothing more than reluctance. She wanted to wait for Lord Richmond, wanted to remain close to the door so that she could be amongst the first to greet him, so that he would know that he was not alone this evening. So that he would know that he had friends present.

But, of course, there was nothing for her to do but return to her chaperone, doing all she could to appear pleased to meet whichever new gentleman she had now to be introduced to.

～

"Pray tell me that Lord Mansford was more conversational than Lord Bellingham!"

Rebecca laughed at the eager look on Lady

Hayward's face. "Yes, he was a significant improvement," she replied, making certain to keep her gaze trained solely on Lady Hayward rather than seek out Lord Richmond, who, she had noticed, had entered the room only a few minutes beforehand. It had taken all of her determination not to study him, not to allow her gaze to linger on him and to, instead, focus entirely on Lord Mansford. She had to admit that Lord Mansford was handsome, engaging, an excellent conversationalist, and was altogether very pleasing indeed. However, she was still thoroughly distracted by Lord Richmond's presence and had been glad when Lord Mansford had excused himself from her company.

"I presume," Lady Hayward said softly, looking at her carefully, "that you have noticed Lord Richmond's arrival?"

A flush crept into Rebecca's face. "Yes, I have," she said, refusing to pretend otherwise.

"And do you wish to speak to him?"

Yet more heat crawled into Rebecca's cheeks. "Lady Hayward," she began, a little embarrassed. "I am taking your advice as best I can. You have instructed me not to further my acquaintance with Lord Richmond, and thus, I have attempted not to do so."

"But you are still very much intrigued by him," Lady Hayward said softly. "Yes, it may have been over a sennight since we met him first in the bookshop, but I have been very well aware that you have found every other gentleman since that meeting to be unsuitable." One eyebrow lifted. "You believe him to be innocent of these rumors, then?"

"I know you do not," Rebecca said hastily, "or, at the very least, you would prefer me not to engage with him to make certain that my reputation remains untarnished."

Lady Hayward let out a long sigh and rubbed one hand lightly across her forehead. "And yet despite that, you appear to be quite fascinated with him," she said softly. "There is an interest there that has not been present with any other gentleman."

Knowing that it was pointless to even attempt to argue with this, Rebecca said nothing but held Lady Hayward's gaze steadily, wondering if there was yet more for the lady to say. Would she continue to encourage her to remain away from Lord Richmond? Or was there any possibility at all that a further acquaintance might be possible?

A long sigh escaped from Lady Hayward as though considering what was next to do. The conversations continued on all around them but Rebecca remained silent, her heart quickening a little more as Lady Hayward bit her lip.

"I have always encouraged you to find a gentleman that strikes an interest in your heart, have I not?" Lady Hayward said eventually. "Why it should be this particular gentleman, I do not know, but there is clearly something about him that has captured your interest. Therefore," she continued, a little more quietly, "I shall remain by your side and will permit you a further conversation with him this evening. Thereafter, I shall consider the matter a little longer." A glimmer of a smile appeared on her lips. "Perhaps I was a little hasty in my judgment of him."

Rebecca reached out and pressed one hand to Lady Hayward's arm. "I am sorry," she said honestly. "I do not know what it is about Lord Richmond that intrigues me so. It must be very frustrating indeed to have someone such as I as your charge!"

This brought a broad smile to Lady Hayward's face. "Not at all, my dear," she replied warmly. "Although I am glad that your sisters are not present this evening, else I do not think I should have been able to permit you such a thing!" She smiled and tilted her head just a little. "Shall we go and speak with him now?"

Rebecca nodded, and slowly, the two ladies walked together across the room. It took some minutes for them to reach Lord Richmond, who was, Rebecca saw, standing rather far away from the other guests and conversing quietly with their host. Rebecca saw how he shifted from foot to foot, how his gaze darted from here to there as though he were deeply worried about who might approach him.

"Good evening, Lord Richmond."

Both Lord Merrick and Lord Richmond turned towards them at once, and Rebecca bobbed a quick curtsy, seeing the slight widening of Lord Richmond's eyes as he lifted his head from his bow.

"Good evening, Lady Hayward, Lady Rebecca," both gentlemen said before Lord Merrick, perhaps sensing that they wanted to speak to Lord Richmond, quickly took his leave.

"I must admit to being surprised that you wished to speak to me, Lady Hayward," Lord Richmond continued quietly, looking at Lady Hayward directly. "Although I will not say I am not glad."

Lady Hayward smiled and spread her hands. "I am, I confess, a little chagrined, Lord Richmond. I spoke harshly to you when I realize now I ought not to have done. I am, of course, doing all I can to protect Lady Rebecca's reputation."

"*Most* understandable," Lord Richmond replied, finally looking towards Rebecca, who found a strange flurry of excitement rushing through her as she smiled back at him. "And yet you permit another conversation with me, Lady Hayward?" His eyes returned to Rebecca's chaperone. "Is that wise?"

Rebecca found herself speaking before she realized what she was doing. "You are very kind to think of me with such consideration, Lord Richmond," she said, aware of the warmth in her cheeks, "but as I have said, I am quite determined to believe your words rather than listen to the gossip that runs so wildly throughout London." She smiled at him again. "I think you would appreciate a few more welcoming acquaintances, would you not?"

Lord Richmond chuckled, his face lighting up to reveal a most pleasant manner. His blue eyes appeared brighter, no longer the stormy gray she had seen only moments before. It seemed he would be glad of her company, and that made Rebecca feel all the happier.

"I would be very glad indeed, yes," Lord Richmond agreed as Lady Hayward nodded slowly. "It has been trying, I will admit."

"But it can be nothing more than brief conversations,

Lord Richmond," Lady Hayward said firmly. "Nothing that would bring any overt notice from the *ton*. I am sure you understand."

Lord Richmond nodded. "But of course," he replied, still looking very pleased indeed. "I am very grateful for your consideration, Lady Hayward." His eyes turned towards Rebecca. "And to you, also, Lady Rebecca. It is not very often that one finds a young lady of quality, particularly one on her very first outing within society, so willing to believe a gentleman proclaimed guilty of such things."

There was no reasonable way to explain why she felt such a way, and thus, Rebecca could only remain standing quietly, dropping her eyes to the floor as Lady Hayward cleared her throat gently.

"If you would excuse me for a moment," Lady Hayward murmured, astonishing Rebecca by leaving her standing alone with Lord Richmond. "I must refresh my drink." Giving Rebecca a somewhat firm look, which told her that she would only be a few minutes and that propriety was expected at all times, Lady Hayward took her leave, staying only a few steps away from them both.

Rebecca did not know what to say, allowing her gaze to rest on Lord Richmond and noting that he too appeared a little uncomfortable. His eyes were darting from one side of the room to the next, never quite looking at her as he clasped his hands behind his back and shuffled his feet. This was not as Rebecca had expected. She had hoped that the conversation between them would flow easily, but it seemed that he was just as uncertain as to what to say as she.

"When last we met, you were interested in a particular book," she said, feeling a little foolish. "Tell me, Lord Richmond, are you a great reader?"

Blue eyes met hers, and Lord Richmond gave her a brief shrug. "I should like to be, Lady Rebecca, but I fear I am not," he answered as she smiled up at him. "Unfortunately, I cannot even recall the name of the book I was interested in, Lady Rebecca, else I might have been able to discuss it with you!"

"That does not matter," Rebecca replied quickly. "I am only relieved that we are able to converse again, Lord Richmond. I did not think that Lady Hayward would permit it."

"Again," he replied, his expression gentling as he finally allowed himself to look at her, "I am honored by your belief in me, Lady Rebecca. Particularly when it is entirely unmerited."

She shook her head. "It is not unmerited, Lord Richmond. There are those in society who do not accept what has been said of you. You have friends who know you well. They do not believe the account of such scandalous events. Why should I trust the gossip mongers instead of those who know you better than they?"

Lord Richmond studied her carefully, his eyes searching her face as though seeking some sort of confirmation that she was speaking the truth. And then, after some moments, he sighed and passed one hand over his eyes.

"I am very blessed in your acquaintance, I think," he said softly. "And for that, Lady Rebecca, I thank you. You are taking a risk to your own reputation in even conversing with me."

"And one I am willing to take," Rebecca replied quietly. "Perhaps we might speak again soon, Lord Richmond. Perhaps by then, you will have remembered the name of your book!" Her lips quirked, recalling that she herself was the one who had the book in her possession. This, in turn, made Lord Richmond chuckle, and he inclined his head.

"I should be very glad to do so, Lady Rebecca," he replied with a grin. "But only at an appropriate time." His smile faded a little. "I am sure that you will have a good many acquaintances to speak to otherwise."

"But I shall make certain to seek you out, Lord Richmond," Rebecca said, aware that there was a promise in her words that she would have to fulfill. "On that, I am quite determined."

There was no time for them to say more, for Lady Hayward soon reappeared, and Rebecca was required to excuse herself from Lord Richmond's presence. But she could not hide the smile on her face as she crossed the room, feeling happiness and contentment within her heart that had not been there for some time.

CHAPTER SEVEN

"You see? Not everyone is rejecting you."
Jeffery gave Lord Swinton a sharp glance. "Yes, I am well aware that there are those in society who are glad to have my company still," he said a little doubtfully. "Although some, I am sure, relish the fact that the *beau monde* will talk about their event a little more due to my presence here." This, he was certain, was the case this evening, for the evening assembly was hosted by Lord and Lady Crawford, who were both well known to enjoy speaking of and spreading as many rumors as they could.

Lord Swinton shrugged. "You did not have to attend."

Jeffery knew that such a statement was true but did not allow himself to admit it to his friend. The only reason he had come this evening was the hope that Lady Rebecca might be present, that she might be willing to come and speak to him again. He had not, as yet, told Lord Swinton of what had occurred at the soiree a few evenings ago and, thus far, had no particular eagerness to do so. His friend would, no doubt, find it very interesting indeed and would want to discuss all manner of things before Jeffery himself could think of what such an interest meant.

Lady Rebecca was quite extraordinary in that way. She appeared to be eager to be in his company, even though it was quite clear that to do so could cause difficulties for her own reputation. On top of which, she was remarkably pretty, the daughter of a duke, and was present within society for the sole reason of finding a suitable husband.

But no, he was being foolish. A gentleman with a stained reputation such as he could not even think of pursuing a lady like that. Particularly when her chaperone had made it very clear indeed that there was only to be the briefest of conversations."

"Lord Richmond?"

Jeffery turned, a little surprised to see a footman standing there. Was he about to be asked to leave the evening assembly? Had his hosts changed their minds about his presence here? "Yes?"

"If you might follow me, my lord," the footman said, bowing and gesturing behind him. "There is someone who wishes to speak to you in private."

Jeffery frowned and did not immediately move. "Might I ask who it is?"

The footman's expression did not change. "Lord Merrick, I believe," he said calmly. "There is something of particular urgency."

Immediately, Jeffery excused himself from Lord

Swinton. "I should go at once," he said as Lord Swinton nodded understandingly. "I do hope he is all right."

"I am sure it will be nothing of great importance," Lord Swinton replied encouragingly. "Do come and join me again once your conversation is over." A grin flickered across his face. "I should like to know who or what has been distracting you so greatly these last few minutes."

Jeffery laughed and shook his head before quickly following after the footman. He was led to another door, far from the other guests in a dimly lit part of the house. The footman said nothing further but opened the door for him, standing ready to close it again the moment Jeffery stepped inside.

"Oh, Richmond!"

In an instant, Jeffery knew he had made a mistake. The familiar voice that reached him was not that of Lord Merrick. Instead, it was that of Lady Kensington, who had risen out of her chair and was now standing with her hands held out towards him, her eyes fixed to his.

Fear swam in his belly. If he was discovered, then his reputation as a rogue and a scoundrel would be solidified. He would have no choice but to leave London, unable to protest his innocence any longer. A vision of Lady Rebecca came into his mind, pain stabbing his heart as he realized he would have to forget about her entirely, aware of just how much pain he would cause her if caught. She would realize that everything he had said had been a falsehood. There would be no opportunity to explain himself further.

"I want nothing to do with this," he growled, stepping

back from her and towards the door again. "You should not have done this, Lady Kensington."

"Oh, please, Lord Richmond!" Tears sparkled in her eyes, but Jeffery shook his head and pulled at the door handle.

It did not open.

He tried again but it remained fixed in place. Closing his eyes, he took in a steadying breath before turning back to Lady Kensington, anger ripping through him now.

"Have your man open this door at once!" he demanded as Lady Kensington remained precisely where she was, looking entirely woebegone. "I will not stand for this, Lady Kensington!"

The tears faded from her eyes in an instant and, in that instant, Jeffery realized that it had been nothing more than an act. She sniffed once, delicately, before turning her head and looking towards the large windows that showed nothing but the clear night sky.

"You have ruined everything for me, Lord Richmond," she said, her voice thin and flat as Jeffery fought to control his temper. "If you had only accepted my affections as you ought, then Lord Kensington would not have discovered us. I would have taken you to another room, to another place, where we would not have been disturbed. Your reputation would have remained intact and I would have gained what I have long desired."

Jeffery shook his head, disgusted with her. "I do not simply do as you wish, Lady Kensington," he said darkly. "It is not my fault that there have been consequences for your actions."

She turned sharply to him, her eyes now a little

narrowed. "Lord Kensington will barely allow me from his sight," she said, her voice low. "Fortunately, this evening, he has been forced to depart from the house to deal with a serious business matter. Promising him that I would remain at home until he returned, I quickly prepared to depart, knowing that you had been invited here this evening."

Jeffery snorted. "Lady Crawford is one of your close acquaintances, I presume."

"She is indeed," Lady Kensington replied without hesitation. "And she has given me the opportunity to speak with you so that my difficulties do not continue."

A hard laugh escaped Jeffery's lips. "Your difficulties are your own, Lady Kensington. I have nothing to do with them."

Shaking her head, she spread her hands. "You are, unfortunately, the sole reason for such a thing," she said with such a false sweetness that Jeffery turned away from her, no longer even able to look into her face. "If you had given me what I wished, then we might be just as we were. Just as we should be. And because you did not, there are consequences for us both."

"Consequences I will bear," Jeffery spat, rounding on her. "Consequences that have come from my choosing what is right over what *you* might wish for, Lady Kensington. I am determined to show society I am not what they believe me to be, that I am *not* this scoundrel who does the things as they say of me. Whether they believe me or not is yet to be seen, but I am determined to prove it."

Lady Kensington tipped her head, looking at him in a

bird-like fashion. Her eyes ran over his frame before returning to his face, and Jeffery's stomach twisted. She was much more calculating than he had ever realized before, much darker in her considerations than he had ever perceived. And now he felt as though he were caught up in her schemes without having had any intention of being so trapped.

"Your reputation means nothing to me, Lord Richmond," Lady Kensington began, her voice silk, her words like gentle caresses despite the harsh, cruel words that were being spoken. "I am entirely without sympathy for where you stand at present. In fact, I intend to make it all the more difficult."

Jeffery's stomach dropped but he did not move an inch. Instead, his frame stiffened, his eyes narrowed, and his hands slowly curled tightly into fists.

"You will not ask me what my intentions are?" Lady Kensington teased, her smile crooked and uninviting. "Very well, I shall tell you." She took another step closer to him, her skirts rustling gently, and Jeffery felt himself begin to slide into a waiting darkness that was entirely impossible to escape from.

Lady Kensington waited for another few moments, allowing his torment to linger before she spoke again.

"I intend, Lord Richmond, to punish you for what you have done," she said. "You have, it seems, escaped severe consequences from the *ton* as there are those within the *beau monde* who simply refuse to believe that you could *ever* have attempted to steal affections from another man's wife." Her lip curled in either anger or distaste and Jeffery turned on his heel, refusing to look at her and instead making his way back to the door. He yanked at the door handle once, twice, but still, it would not budge.

Behind him, Lady Kensington laughed. "The door will not be open to you until I have finished what I have to say," she said as though it was all nothing more than some sort of delicious enticement she was enjoying every moment of. "Your efforts are entirely fruitless, Richmond."

Jeffery closed his eyes but did not turn back to her. "I am not required to listen."

"Oh yes, you are," came the swift response. "For unless you *very* much wish the consequences to fall upon those around you, those whom you consider your friends, then I suggest you pay attention to every single word I have to say."

Closing his eyes tightly, Jeffery removed his hand from the door handle but did not turn around. An edge of fear had come into his heart now, wondering just which of his friends Lady Kensington now spoke of.

"Lord Swinton is a *very* dear friend of yours, I know," Lady Kensington continued, her voice softer than before as though she were trying to speak in such a way so as not to injure him further. "Lord and Lady Merrick seem to be eager to help you in any way they can. And, for whatever reason, that young lady, the daughter of the Duke of Landon, seems quite intent on being in your company."

Jeffery's stomach dropped, a heavy weight landing on his shoulders as he forced himself to steady his breathing. Whatever Lady Kensington had planned, it was clear now that she had those within society willing to help her.

There was no reasonable way for her to know of Lady Rebecca on her own.

"You will not say anything?" Lady Kensington teased. "What a shame. I had thought you might try to defend the latter, at the very least, since she has not long been in your company."

A hard response came to his lips, but Jeffery pushed it away at once, refusing to allow himself a single word. It would be best to allow her to speak as she wished, to say all that she wanted but without responding to her at all. That was surely the quickest way to remove himself from this situation and return to the evening assembly.

"They will all come into difficulty unless you do as I ask," Lady Kensington continued quietly. "I will not continue to live under my husband's dictates, Lord Richmond. *You* are the sole cause of such a thing being put into place, for you did not give into your eagerness to be close to me when such an opportunity was presented. When you behaved in such a way, my husband discovered us, and since that moment, has barely allowed me from his sight. That will not be permitted to continue."

"Then you expect me now to do as you bid me?" Jeffery asked, incredulous as he turned back to look at her. "Somehow, you believe that you will simply say a word and I will obey you?"

Lady Kensington's smile was dark. "But of course," she said with a small shrug. "Else I will bring scandal into the lives of every one of your dear friends." Her voice dropped to barely a whisper, and a shudder ran up Jeffery's spine. "Lord Swinton will find himself in a mire of trouble, Lord and Lady Merrick will have their marriage set asunder by the lies of another. And Lady Rebecca..." She smiled, and Jeffery's heart began to pound with worry. "Lady Rebecca will find her reputation so badly damaged that she will not be able to turn her head in society without someone whispering about her."

Jeffery closed his eyes. There appeared to be no way for him to escape from such a thing and yet everything in him wanted to defy her, wanted to refuse and to step away from the lady at once. But dare he risk it? Dare to put his friends and Lady Rebecca into such danger?

"Lady Rebecca is a mere acquaintance," he said a little throatily. "There is no need to involve her in any of your threats."

Lady Kensington only laughed. "Oh, but I think there is," she said after a few moments. "You could warn Lord Swinton. You could speak openly to Lord and Lady Merrick about what I intend. But you could not do so to Lady Rebecca. Not when your acquaintance has only just begun, not when she has placed so much trust in you after only a few short conversations." She laughed again, and Jeffery knew she had won. "You would be driving her away from you for good, should you do such a thing. And even if you chose to do so, even if you decided that it would be best for you to warn them all about what I have threatened, you can be certain that such consequences will certainly take place regardless." Her eyes lifted to his, sparkling with her victory. "In short, Lord Richmond, you have nothing left but to agree."

Jeffery shook his head. "I will not," he said harshly,

even though he knew full well he would have to agree. "I cannot allow you to rule over me in such a fashion."

Lady Kensington shrugged carelessly. "Then you condemn your friends and Lady Rebecca," she said calmly. "I will, of course, permit you to think on my words for a short time, but have no doubt, Lord Richmond, my first demand will come very soon. And you will be expected to agree."

She said nothing more but walked to the door, rapping lightly upon it in a pattern, so that the person on the other side would know it was she. Within a few seconds, the door was opened, and Lady Kensington stood to one side, gesturing for Jeffery to make his way through.

"I look forward to writing to you very soon, Lord Richmond," she said warmly, as though they were the very best of friends. "I do hope you will enjoy the rest of the evening."

The door Jeffery had been so desperate to walk through now seemed like a waiting judgment. If he stepped from the room, then he would be allowing Lady Kensington to have spoken her demands without his rebuttal. He would be admitting to her that the words she had said now were fixed to his thoughts, that he would, in fact, consider them and permit himself to think on what she asked. If he remained, however, Jeffery knew that nothing more would come of it. With the door now open wide, there was every chance that someone from the *ton* would walk past and see both himself and Lady Kensington within—and then where would he be?

The laugh that rang from Lady Kensington's voice as

he walked by her made the hairs stand up on the back of Jeffery's neck. He despised her for what she had done, hated the words she had spoken and the demands she now made—and yet, to his befuddled and muddy mind, there appeared no way for him to escape from such a thing. If he were to protect his friends, to protect Lady Rebecca, then he would have to do as she asked.

And what will she ask? he thought to himself, returning to where he had left Lord Swinton and picking up a glass of brandy as he went. He dared not want to even think about what such a consequence might be, too afraid to even consider the possibilities. She had spoken of punishment, of consequence for him, and now Jeffery's shoulders were so heavy with his burden that he felt as though he were being slowly crushed by it.

"Ah, there you are!"

The bright, cheerful voice of Lord Swinton was in hard contrast to the battle going on within Jeffery's head.

"How was Lord Merrick?" Lord Swinton asked as music and laughter and conversation began to swirl all around Jeffery again, making him feel as though he were stood apart from it all, under a black shroud that forced him away from everyone else. Would they be able to see the cloud he stood under, should they look at him? Would it be apparent that he was in a deep torment?

"I say, Richmond, is something the matter?"

Jeffery looked back at his friend with dull eyes, his brow furrowing as he shook his head.

"Something *is* the matter," Lord Swinton continued, now looking very concerned indeed. "Is it Lord Merrick?

Has something happened to him?" He moved a little closer to Jeffery. "Or is it Lady Merrick? I do hope she—"

"Lord Merrick was not there."

The words burned on Jeffery's lips as he spoke, his head dropping low as he tried to decide whether or not he ought to speak of this all to his friend.

"What do you mean?" Lord Swinton asked, now looking all the more confused. "Lord Merrick was not present? But the footman said—"

"I—I need to think," Jeffery interrupted, rubbing one hand across his forehead before he threw back his brandy, swallowing the measure in one large gulp. Heat spread through his chest, and he accepted it gladly, wishing that it would clear his mind rather than confuse it further.

Lord Swinton's mouth was a little ajar as he stared back at Jeffery, clearly now all too aware that something was very wrong indeed.

"Perhaps to Whites."

"I will go with you, of course," Lord Swinton said slowly, reaching out to put one hand on Jeffery's arm as though he feared he might suddenly faint. "Whatever has been said, it is clearly of great consequence."

"Good evening, Lord Richmond!"

Before he could prevent it, a loud groan escaped from Jeffery's lips as he turned his head, seeing the shock immediately jump onto the features of Lady Rebecca and Lady Hayward. Lady Rebecca's face went from white to crimson in only a few moments, leaving Jeffery struggling to explain himself, noting out of the corner of his eye Lady Rebecca's two sisters, who stood talking together whilst watching him with suspicious eyes.

"There has been some severe news," he heard Lord Swinton express as he himself struggled to find what he might say to Lady Rebecca. "Lord Richmond has only just heard it."

"I see," Lady Hayward replied, a tightness about her lips that had not been there only moments before. "I do hope all is well, Lord Richmond."

Jeffery took in a long breath and forced himself to speak calmly. "You are very kind, Lady Hayward," he said slowly, suddenly wondering which of Lady Kensington's friends would be watching such an interaction so that she might then tell the lady thereafter. "It has been something of a shock."

"I am sorry to hear it," Lady Rebecca replied, her eyes searching his face as he glanced at her. "I had thought to come and converse with you this evening for a short while, but perhaps now is not the best time to do so."

Jeffery did not answer, only for Lord Swinton to clear his throat and elbow him hard in the ribs, shifting his stance just a little so as to cover his actions. Jeffery gave himself a slight shake, looking into the concerned eyes of Lady Rebecca and trying his best to speak with both consideration and appreciation.

"Your concern is appreciated, Lady Rebecca," he said, inclining his head. "What was it you wished to speak of?"

She looked thoroughly confused. "Whatever came to mind," she replied as Lady Hayward and Lord Swinton began to speak quietly. "But if you are troubled, then I must make certain not to disturb you."

Jeffery closed his eyes again, remembering the harsh

words of Lady Kensington and finding himself drawing close to despair. He wanted desperately to linger in Lady Rebecca's presence, wanted urgently to converse with her, to see her smile and to speak with an openness of heart that he had not yet had with any young lady of his acquaintance. And yet to do so would be to put her in a little more danger, given just what Lady Kensington had threatened.

"I think, Lady Rebecca, that for the moment, it might be best for you to step away from me," he said bluntly. "I do not mean to cause you ill nor to appear ungrateful for your willingness to befriend me and to speak to me when within society, but there are matters at hand that could endanger your reputation all the more."

"And I have told you that I am willing to take such a risk," Lady Rebecca said firmly, but Jeffery shook his head.

"I am not," he replied as her eyes flared for a moment, spots of color lingering on her cheeks. "Your reputation, your character, and your sweetness of heart are all much too important, of too much consequence for me to allow them to be trampled for my sake, Lady Rebecca."

He watched as her color heightened, clearly caught between appreciation of his remark and frustration at being told she could no longer be so acquainted with him. He could not blame her for her confusion, given that only two days prior, he had been thankful and eager for her continued acquaintance and now was telling her that, instead, there ought to be nothing further between them. One moment he had been pulling her towards him, the next, pushing her away.

"Lord Richmond," Lady Rebecca said softly, moving just a little closer and looking up into his eyes. "Something has happened, has it not?"

He looked away. "Please, Lady Rebecca."

"Something that is deeply troubling, no doubt," she continued, ignoring him. "You are not alone in this, Lord Richmond. You need not push me away. You know very well that I am glad to be acquainted with you." Her eyes flickered. "Are we never to have the opportunity to know each other a little better?"

He took a deep breath, remembering with horror what Lady Kensington had threatened. "As much as I might wish to, Lady Rebecca," he said honestly, "to give in to all that I might seek will only cause you trouble."

"Trouble that I might be willing to accept," she said, but Jeffery reached out and grasped her hand, squeezing it tightly. Lady Rebecca caught her breath, her eyes widening, and Jeffery found he could not speak for a moment, his own heart thundering furiously at the touch of her hand in his.

"Trouble I will refuse to place upon you, Lady Rebecca," he said, hoarsely. "Leave me. Do not come to seek me out again, I beg you. For your own sake, you must do this."

She did not immediately respond, her fingers shifting slightly, her thumb running over the back of his hand. Jeffery swallowed hard, aware of the way his heart was exploding in his chest, wanting desperately to pursue her, to be able to seek her out as he might do with any other lady of his acquaintance, but knowing full well he could not.

"What if I cannot, Lord Richmond?" she asked as he dropped his head. "What then?"

"You must," he replied, reluctantly letting go of her hand. "There is no other choice for you, Lady Rebecca. Save yourself before you become all the more entangled in the web that surrounds me."

There was a faint glow in her eyes as she looked back at him, her lips pressed hard together and a determination seeming to emanate from her. Jeffery could feel his resolve slipping away and knew that if she did not leave his presence soon, he would, most likely, tell her to forget all that he had said in favor of her remaining in his company.

"Lady Rebecca, let us take our leave."

Jeffery turned to Lady Hayward with a start, having quite forgotten her presence. To hide his reaction, he bowed quickly towards her but did not miss the knowing gleam in her eye.

"Good evening, Lady Hayward, and I thank you for coming to speak to me," he said honestly as Lord Swinton frowned hard behind her. "I hope you both enjoy what is left of the assembly."

"I am sure we will," Lady Hayward replied as Lady Rebecca bobbed a quick curtsy in farewell. "May whatever is troubling you soon be resolved, Lord Richmond."

He gave her a brief smile before turning his gaze back towards Lady Rebecca, who was still watching him, a troubled look in her eyes. "Good evening, Lady Rebecca," he rumbled, feeling as though he was saying a pronounced farewell. "May the remaining months of the Season be a great success."

She said nothing, frowned hard, and then turned her head away, moving past him so that she might rejoin her sisters, who had been waiting patiently for them to finish their conversation. Jeffery sighed and ran one hand over his face before looking back to his friend.

"To Whites, Swinton?" he asked, praying that he would quickly agree. "I do not think I can linger here any longer."

Lord Swinton nodded without hesitation. "But of course," he replied, curiosity clear in his eyes. "At once, if you wish."

"At once," Jeffery repeated before turning on his heel and making his way through the crowd, suddenly desperate to remove himself from the evening assembly and find the fresh air that would allow him freedom from the trouble that had thrown itself at him, clinging to him now with such a weight that Jeffery felt as though he were being pulled down into the ground, his steps heavy and his spirits low. It seemed that he would have no other choice but to obey Lady Kensington, no matter what it cost him. To refuse would be unthinkable.

CHAPTER EIGHT

"Good afternoon, Lord Clayton."
Rebecca smiled back at the handsome gentleman as he bent over her hand, relieved beyond expression that this was to be the final visit for this afternoon. Behind her, she could hear one of her sisters giggle—although she could guess which one it was.

"I do hope I might be permitted to call upon you again, Lady Rebecca," Lord Clayton said, one eyebrow lifting towards the duke who sat quietly in his chair, seemingly bored with the conversation. Rebecca glanced at her father, who quickly rose to his feet and cleared his throat in a harsh manner.

"Yes, yes, of course," he said quickly as Rebecca kept her smile fixed in place. "You would be very welcome indeed, Lord Clayton. Good afternoon."

The two gentlemen exchanged farewells and Rebecca waited until Lord Clayton had left the room before she sat back down in her chair, albeit a little too heavily, for her father noticed at once and lifted an eyebrow in her direction.

"Not suitable for you, then?" he queried as Rebecca smiled. "He is only an earl, I suppose."

"A handsome earl!" Lady Selina interrupted, one hand flying to her mouth as both she and Lady Anna giggled. The duke, perhaps uncertain as to what to do with such silly creatures as his daughters, ignored them entirely.

"I did give him permission to call upon you again, however," he continued, looking at Rebecca with one lifted brow. "I do hope that you will entertain him, although, of course, should someone with a more suitable title come to call, then you can easily make your disinterest in Lord Clayton plain."

Rebecca smiled to herself. "Yes, Father," she said quietly as the duke nodded, clearly satisfied with himself that he had guided his daughter so well. "I believe I have one more caller this afternoon, although I cannot be certain of when he will arrive." She glanced towards her sisters, who were now looking at her with interest. "My sisters can sit with me, of course."

The duke frowned. "Lady Hayward should be here," he muttered as Rebecca remained quiet. "If only she had not that unfortunate meeting with her solicitors, I would not have to do—"

"We can sit with Rebecca, Father," Lady Selina interrupted brightly, smiling eagerly at her father as she repeated Rebecca's words. "That is quite proper, particularly since there are two of us who will be present."

"*More* than proper," Lady Anna agreed as Rebecca

held her father's gaze steadily. "And we will not leave the room or do anything foolish."

"I am sure you have plenty to attend to, Father," Rebecca said gently. "Please, there is no need to linger."

The duke harrumphed, then nodded. "Very well," he said, much to Rebecca's relief. "You are to attend the fashionable hour in Hyde Park, I understand?"

Rebecca nodded. "Lady Hayward is to call for us soon, Father," she acknowledged. "I will make sure to inform you before we depart."

This seemed to satisfy the duke, for he exited the room without another word or even a backward glance, leaving his daughters to sit together as they had done so many times before. Rebecca let out a long breath and looked to her sisters, who were sitting quietly, although with an expectant look on their faces.

It was time to take them into her confidence.

"I am hopeful that Lord Swinton and Lord Richmond will call," Rebecca said quickly, praying that there was nothing about that name on her lips that would affect her expression. "I do not think that father is aware of the gossip surrounding Lord Richmond, but, if he is, it would be best if he did not remain in the room when they come to call." Her heart twisted in her chest, uncertain as to whether or not Lord Richmond would be willing to attend. He had been very clear in his decision last evening and whilst she had been required to step away from him, she had felt that same urgency to remain in his company, to speak at length with him and to find out the truth of what was now pushing him from her once more.

Lord Swinton had agreed at once, his note received

by her within the hour of her first sending the invitation. Of Lord Richmond, however, she could not be certain, and it was this that made her all the more anxious.

"Lord Richmond?" Lady Selina repeated, a look of astonishment etched on her features. "But he is a rake, Rebecca!"

"He is not," Rebecca replied firmly. "He has been mistaken for a rake. It was a mixup. There are those within society who do not believe the rumors. I will state now... I am one of them."

"Is Lady Hayward aware of his intention to call?" Lady Anna asked, sounding a little doubtful. "I am sure she would have something to say on the matter if she were aware of it."

"As you saw last evening," Rebecca said primly, "she permitted me to converse with him and, I am certain, would not be against his visit this afternoon."

She watched as her sisters looked at each other before returning their gaze to Rebecca. Both of them looked doubtful indeed, although Rebecca did not feel the need to defend herself any further. They did not need to know that it had been she who had written to both Lord Swinton and Lord Richmond and invited them to call. In fact, Rebecca considered, the less they were aware of, the better.

"I am not certain I would be glad to share company with Lord Richmond, Rebecca," Lady Anna said slowly, her brow suddenly furrowing. "What if he—"

A scratch at the door interrupted them, and Rebecca rose to her feet at once, her heart hammering furiously as the butler came in. Had he come? Had he agreed to see her once more, even though he had spoken with such evident determination last evening?

"Lord Swinton, my lady," the butler said, glancing at Lady Anna and Lady Selina as though making certain she was not alone. "And Lord Richmond."

Rebecca swallowed hard, her nervousness beginning to climb up within her. "But of course," she said quickly. "Some tea trays, if you please."

The butler nodded, and, in a moment, both Lord Swinton and Lord Richmond were bowing towards the three ladies, with Lord Richmond looking all about the room as though he had expected Lady Hayward to be present.

"My father has had to return to his business affairs," Rebecca said, by way of explanation. "Please, do be seated." She gestured to two chairs, and, much to her relief, Lord Swinton stepped forward at once and took the seat closest to her two sisters. They both blushed furiously at his warm and charming smile, engaging him quickly in conversation and leaving Rebecca free to speak to Lord Richmond.

"Lord Richmond," Rebecca murmured, seeing the way that he sat down almost gingerly in a chair, as if uncertain as to whether or not he would be welcome. "You were willing to call."

Blue eyes reached hers. "I am still uncertain about my visit, Lady Rebecca," he said gruffly. "But I find that the thought of refusing such an invitation is much too painful."

Rebecca's heart quickened. Was he trying to tell her that he too was drawn to her much in the way that she felt drawn to him? It was such an inexplicable feeling, and Rebecca could not even find the words to truly express it, but a flicker of hope burned within her heart as she looked into his eyes, seeing both misery and happiness there.

"And what of your troubles, Lord Richmond?" she asked softly. "Are they still as great as last evening?"

He nodded. "Worse, in fact," he told her. "But I shall not bring them to your attention, Lady Rebecca. What I will say is that I do not feel I can be in your company in such a way as this very often, even if I find myself all the more eager to do so."

Her lips curved into an immediate smile as Lord Richmond looked away, seeming a little self-conscious. "You mean to say that you wish to further our acquaintance?"

Lord Richmond sighed and raised one hand to his eyes before dropping it again. "I—I do, Lady Rebecca," he admitted. "I find myself thinking of you often, and, even though we are not particularly well acquainted, I cannot help but..." Trailing off, he gave her a small, rueful smile. "I try my best to protect you, Lady Rebecca, and then the next moment, I do the very opposite of what I know would be best."

"I am glad you do," Rebecca told him, quietly, so that her sisters would not overhear—although, given the laughter that came from them, she did not think that they were even paying attention to her. "Are you able to tell me what troubles you so? I would be glad to do what I can to help."

Immediately, Lord Richmond held up both hands.

"I cannot," he said firmly. "I *will* not. My troubles are not for your ears, Lady Rebecca. All I wish to do at present is converse with you as any other gentleman might." His expression softened, and he dropped his hands. "To pretend that I have no other difficulties at present."

Rebecca smiled back at him, for whilst this was not the resolve she had wanted, it was satisfactory to her. "Very well," she agreed quietly. "Then let us converse, Lord Richmond. What is it you would like to speak of?"

He chuckled. "Books," he said with a grin. "I have recalled the name of the novel I found so interesting the first day we met, Lady Rebecca."

"Oh?" Her hand reached for something tucked down the side of her chair, finding it and then quickly pulling it free. "Might it be this?" A laugh escaped her at the astonishment in his face, the way his eyes widened as she handed him the very book he had been about to mention. The conversation to her right lapsed for a moment, only to resume quickly as Lord Swinton continued the discussion with her sisters. Rebecca's smile remained as Lord Richmond stared down at the book before lifting his eyes to hers.

"I have read it," she confessed as Lord Richmond shook his head in evident astonishment. "I thought, mayhap, once you also have done so, we might then be able to discuss it together."

"I see," Lord Richmond murmured, still clearly astonished by what she had done. "That is very kind of you, Lady Rebecca. I am touched by your thoughtfulness."

Her heart lifted. "Something to pull you from your

current troubles, mayhap?" she asked gently. "A way to escape."

Lord Richmond let out a long breath, nodded, and smiled at her again. "Indeed," he agreed softly. "Thank you, Lady Rebecca. I am very grateful, indeed."

THE VISIT WAS OVER MUCH TOO QUICKLY, and Rebecca rose to her feet as the two gentlemen came to take their leave.

"Good afternoon, Lord Richmond," she said, bobbing a quick curtsy. "I hope it will not be too long before we can speak so again."

Lord Richmond opened his mouth as though he wanted to agree with her, only to lapse quickly into silence. Behind her, Lord Swinton was taking his leave of her sisters, and Rebecca knew she only had a few moments left with Lord Richmond.

"Perhaps you might call again," she suggested, knowing that she was speaking much more boldly than any young lady ought. "Or we shall meet at the ball tomorrow evening?"

Sighing heavily, Lord Richmond dropped his head and then lifted it, looking back towards her. "We must be cautious, Lady Rebecca," he said quietly. "I can make no promises to you. Society is still against me, and I fear what will happen to you should you be seen too often in my company." A small smile lifted one corner of his mouth. "But yes, I should be glad to see you again at the ball tomorrow evening."

"And might you be bold enough to dance with me?" she asked, aware of the heat that rushed into her face as she spoke. "If Lady Hayward permits, of course."

He hesitated, clear concern written in his features. "I will consider it, Lady Rebecca," he promised, eventually, as Lord Swinton came to take his leave from her. "Good afternoon."

A swirl of both disappointment and hope rose within her as she bid farewell to both gentlemen. Watching them as they left, her breath hitched as Lord Richmond glanced over his shoulder towards her, a smile spreading across his face for a moment before he turned his head away and finally left the room.

"Rebecca!"

She turned quickly to see both sisters looking at her with wide eyes.

"Yes?" she asked, trying to keep her voice calm. "Whatever is the matter?"

Lady Anna laughed as Lady Selina rolled her eyes.

"We are not blind, Rebecca!" she exclaimed as Rebecca blushed. "Lord Richmond was clearly quite taken with you."

"Nonsense," Rebecca replied with a wave of her hand. "It is only that he and I did not wish to interrupt the conversation that both of you were having with Lord Swinton." She arched one eyebrow. "He appeared to be very taken with the both of you, in fact!"

Pink rose in Lady Selina's cheeks, but Rebecca's words did not seem to influence Lady Anna in any way.

"Now you are being ridiculous," she declared stoutly.

"And you will have to inform Lady Hayward of his interest, Rebecca. She must know of such things."

Panic began to surge in Rebecca's chest. "I hardly think that is necessary," she said quickly. "Unless you wish to inform her of every gentleman that has called this afternoon?"

Lady Anna frowned but said nothing more, looking to her sister for support but, much to Rebecca's relief, Lady Selina merely rose to her feet and then made her way to the door.

"We should prepare for the fashionable hour," she said mildly, looking back over her shoulder. "Lady Hayward will be here very soon."

Rebecca smiled and followed after her. "Yes, of course," she agreed, leaving Lady Anna to trail after them both, her expression one of frustration that the discussion had come to an end. "I should not like to be tardy."

Hurrying back to her room, Rebecca felt her heart lift as she remembered all that she had discussed with Lord Richmond. It had felt quite effortless, as though there had been no difficulties with his situation whatsoever, as if they had been two people within society talking for the mere pleasure of it. She hoped desperately that he would be willing to speak to her again tomorrow evening, although she had been, perhaps, foolish in her suggestion of dancing with him. For the moment, that pleasure would have to wait.

∽

"The fashionable hour is not one of my favorite

occasions, I must confess!" Lady Hayward laughed as Rebecca pressed close to her to avoid three young ladies who were walking together, their chaperones trailing behind them and seeming to ignore all those around them. "How do you fare, Lady Rebecca?"

"Very well, I think," Rebecca replied a little doubtfully, looking all around her and wondering whether or not anyone was taking notice of their presence here this afternoon. "I did not expect it to be so busy!"

Behind her, she heard Lady Anna laugh. "But it is meant to be a crush, Rebecca!" she said mischievously. "But the point is that we are amongst the rest of the *ton* so that our presence might be noted!"

Rebecca glanced over her shoulder at her sister. "I can see why you do not appreciate the fashionable hour, Lady Hayward," she said a little awkwardly. "Although I am glad to be here."

Lady Hayward chuckled, then looped her arm through Rebecca's. "I had hoped to introduce you to an earl who I thought to be most appropriate, but I do not think we shall find him here this afternoon!" She looked across at Rebecca. "Although, no doubt, you shall find something about him to dislike!"

"I shall not agree," Rebecca replied stoutly. "Only this afternoon, Lord Clayton called upon me and I told him I would be glad to see him again." That was not the entirety of the truth, however, and Rebecca felt a small smattering of guilt hit hard against her. "If this earl is pleasing, then I am sure I shall have no concern whatsoever."

"But he shall not be as intriguing as Lord Richmond,

no doubt," Lady Hayward replied with a knowing look. "After what was said last evening, I do not think that you will have simply forgotten him!"

Rebecca let out a small sigh. "You know me much too well, Lady Hayward," she answered with a wry smile. "Yes, I confess that I am still very interested in the gentleman. In fact, he—"

"Good gracious, can that be you, Lady Hayward?"

Rebecca saw Lady Hayward frown as she turned her head to the right and then to the left before sucking in a breath, realizing who it was that had called her name. Rebecca, not recognizing the lady, remained silent and stood by Lady Hayward's side, as did her sisters.

"Good afternoon, Lady Kensington," Lady Hayward said, and instantly, Rebecca stiffened. "I do hope you are enjoying the fine weather this afternoon."

Lady Kensington laughed and fluttered her fan as though the warmth of the afternoon was too much for her.

"Yes, it is *very* enjoyable to be amongst society," Lady Kensington said with a sigh, looking all around her before returning her gaze to Rebecca. "Now, you *must* introduce me to your charges, Lady Hayward. I have heard so much about the duke's daughters that have graced society with their presence!"

Rebecca blinked, a little surprised at the hint of vitriol that was in the lady's words. She dared not say anything, however, leaving Lady Hayward to quickly make the introductions. From the flash in Lady Hayward's eyes, however, Rebecca knew that she was less than willing to do so but had no other choice in the matter, given the circumstances.

"How very good to meet you," Rebecca murmured, dropping into a quick curtsy as Lady Kensington merely inclined her head. Her sisters murmured the same as Lady Kensington looked directly at Rebecca again, her eyes a little narrowed with some sort of spite that Rebecca did not quite understand.

"You are much spoken of in society, Lady Rebecca," Lady Kensington said a little too loudly. "You must be very grateful for Lady Hayward's guiding hand."

Rebecca nodded. "Yes, of course," she said softly, wondering at this state of questioning. "I have been very glad for her, as my sisters have also been." Lady Anna and Lady Selina both murmured their agreement quickly as Lady Hayward smiled tightly.

"Society can so quickly turn on you," Lady Kensington said as though warning Rebecca of something. "I should be very careful indeed, Lady Rebecca."

Lady Hayward cleared her throat gently. "I am quite certain that Lady Rebecca shall do very well in society, indeed," she said, a little sharply. "She has made an excellent first impression and will continue to do so."

Rebecca swallowed hard, a little uncertain as to why Lady Kensington had spoken so. Had Rebecca done something to upset her in some way, even though they had not been introduced until this moment? Or was there a warning there? A warning for Rebecca to be careful as she mixed with the *ton*, even though she was safe and secure with the guidance of Lady Hayward?

"A single word whispered by one to another can start

something truly terrible," Lady Kensington said with a shake of her head as another sigh left her lips. "A single action can affect the rest of your life, Lady Rebecca. It can steal your future, your happiness, and your reputation, plunging you into great misery." Another shake of her head accompanied this, although Rebecca felt nothing more than fright, completely unable to understand why Lady Kensington should speak so. "I should be very upset indeed if such a thing should happen to you."

"It will not," Lady Hayward said decisively, taking a small step in front of Rebecca so that Lady Kensington was forced to look at her rather than keep her gaze fixed to Rebecca. "Now, if you will excuse us, Lady Kensington, there are others we must greet."

With a sweep of her skirts, Lady Kensington stepped aside and lowered her head as though she were some sort of subject and Lady Hayward a great noble. With a tight nod, Lady Hayward moved away from Lady Kensington, taking Rebecca, Anna, and Selina with her.

"Have you ever spoken to her before, Lady Rebecca?" Lady Hayward asked, keeping her voice low as they walked across the park, her eyes serious as she looked at Rebecca. "I must know."

"No," Rebecca said, shaking her head. "No, I have never met the lady before, Lady Hayward. I can assure you of that."

Lady Hayward bit her lip then gave herself a slight shake. "I do not like Lady Kensington," she said bluntly. "But what she said to you was very strange indeed. I do not know what she means, nor do I understand why it was directed at you."

Rebecca let out a slow breath, aware that she had been frightened by Lady Kensington's warning words. She had no knowledge of what the lady had meant nor why she had been spoken to in such a direct manner. Swallowing hard, she took in a steadying breath before speaking again.

"There is nothing to fear, surely," she said softly as Lady Hayward looked at her. "If I am with you as my chaperone, or with my father, then there is nothing I need to be anxious about."

This seemed to buoy Lady Hayward's spirits a little, for the coldness left her eyes, and she nodded.

"Yes, of course," she said a little more firmly. "You have, as I have said, made an excellent impression upon society thus far. I trust that you will not be tempted to ever step away from your chaperone by a gentleman's pleas." Her eyes narrowed just a fraction. "Not even if it is one that you are inclined towards."

Knowing that she spoke of Lord Richmond, Rebecca flushed but held Lady Hayward's gaze. "Never," she promised, having every intention of doing so. "I shall never do so, Lady Hayward. And on that, you have my word."

CHAPTER NINE

Walking into the ballroom, Jeffery let out a long breath and set his shoulders, keeping his head high and refusing to allow any whispers to affect him in any way. He had been invited here this evening and had accepted, glad to know that Lady Rebecca, as well as a few other friends, would be present to greet him. Not that he had any intention of dancing with Lady Rebecca, even though he desperately wished to. To speak to her was one thing, but to take her in his arms was quite another, even if it would be just to dance. The *beau monde* would take note of it, especially if it were just Lady Rebecca that he danced with.

Keeping to the side, Jeffery continued further into the room but remained in the shadows. There was no need for him to step out into the crowd yet. Most of the *ton* wanted to be seen this evening, whilst he wanted to make certain that his presence was not so obvious. Yes, he had some friends here this evening, but most of the *ton* would watch him with suspicious eyes.

"I thought you might be skulking around here."

Jeffery froze, turning his head to see none other than Lady Kensington approaching him. His heart began to hammer, and he turned away, continuing to walk away from her, but her voice reached out to him again, pulling him back.

"You might wish to consider what you are doing, Lord Richmond," she said in a voice loud enough for him to hear. "My husband believes I am gone to the retiring room, but I will be very glad to tell him that the reason I was tardy in returning to him was entirely because of you."

Her words made Jeffery stop dead, hating that he had no other choice but to do so. The threat was real enough, and the last thing Jeffery needed was for any further difficulty to come his way.

"I told you I would tell you what it is I require of you," Lady Kensington said, her voice now closer to him than before. "It is up to you, of course, whether or not you comply. I should hate to think of what will happen, however, if you do not." A quiet laugh escaped her. "I had the pleasure of being introduced to Lady Rebecca. She is *very* lovely and quite innocent. I do hope that Lady Hayward is able to protect her from the…more difficult parts of the *ton*. There is so much that a young lady can become caught up in accidentally, and I do fear for her safety."

He turned, looking into her beautiful face and finding himself cold. Her smile was warm, her head tilted just a little to the left, but the ice in her gaze sent a shudder through him. Lady Kensington was manipulative, cold, and cruel, and he was thoroughly caught in her trap. She knew that every word she spoke about Lady Rebecca was a sword to his heart, a pain to his chest. Whilst he might be able to warn Lord and Lady Merrick and Lord Swinton of what Lady Kensington had threatened and be assured that they would be much more on their guard, there was not the same degree of difficulty that would come to them as would come to Lady Rebecca, should something occur. Lord and Lady Merrick were already wed and, whilst rumors might abound, they had each other, and there was a certain security in that.

Likewise, Lord Swinton. He was a gentleman of the *ton* and well able to shoulder a whisper or two, should it come to it. Most likely, he would do just as Jeffery was doing at present and remain in society, pushing aside the gossip with a firm determination.

But with Lady Rebecca, there was nothing that could protect her reputation from damage. No matter how well Lady Hayward guided her, no matter how well she behaved, a single mistake or deliberate action by another could ruin her forever. And both he and Lady Kensington knew that.

"What is it that you want, Lady Kensington?" he growled, feeling his hackles rise as she smiled up at him. "I have endured your threats playing about in my mind for some time already, and I will not permit you to continue to do so."

"Then you will not do as I ask?" Lady Kensington asked, sounding a little surprised. She studied him for a few moments as the flickering candlelight sent shadows twisting over their faces before another laugh escaped from her. "No, you will do so because of your affection for Lady Rebecca."

"I have no affection for her," Jeffery stated angrily, "but I will not permit you to ruin her to injure me."

Lady Kensington lifted one shoulder in a half shrug. "I care not," she said flippantly. "I hold you responsible for my present circumstances, as you know, for my husband barely lets me from his sight, and if I am even a few minutes late on my return, he will question me as to where I have been." An ugly expression came to her face, her lip curled, and her eyes filled with a hatred of her situation. "I had to endure a great deal from him after we had spoken, Lord Richmond. Which is why I shall not linger. I shall not tarry here long." A glance over her shoulder betrayed her slight anxiety. "I do expect you to do as I have asked, however, without hesitation."

Jeffery said nothing, his jaw working furiously as he fought to contain all his fiery emotions. He was both angry and upset, furious with himself for agreeing and yet knowing that there was nothing else he could have done. He had to protect Lady Rebecca in any way he could.

"This evening, there is a particular gentleman here that I *very* much wish to speak with later," Lady Kensington continued as Jeffery's stomach dropped. "You will inform him of such. You will tell him that I am, unfortunately, required to remain in my husband's company at present, but you will ask him to call upon me tomorrow afternoon during the fashionable hour." A small smile crept over her face. "When my husband will be absent from the house on business."

Jeffery's stomach turned over on itself, and he closed his eyes, hating the fact that he would have to repeat such words to another gentleman.

"You are not going to ask me who it is I wish to speak to?" Lady Kensington asked teasingly. "You wish very much to remain silent, to show no interest?" She laughed at him, and Jeffery's fingernails bit into his palms, his anger burning all the hotter. "Very well, your resolve, I suppose, does you credit." Taking something from her pocket, she held it out to him. "And give him this so he knows your words can be trusted."

Unwillingly, Jeffery stretched out a hand and took the delicate locket from Lady Kensington. It was of burnished gold, sitting on a delicate chain. He did not want to ask whether or not it was from this particular gentleman, choosing instead just to slip it into his pocket without remark.

"You are determined not to ask me anything, then," Jeffery heard Lady Kensington say as he turned his head away from her, hating every moment of her company. "Very well, very well. Now, you are to find Lord Bellingham. And when you have done so, make certain you inform me of the fact."

"Impossible!" Jeffery retorted, spinning around to face her. "I will not come *near* to you this evening, Lady Kensington."

"Oh yes, you will," she replied calmly. "And you will tell me that it has been done, else I shall go to Lady Rebecca. It would be most unfortunate if—"

"Enough." Jeffery sliced the air with his hand, cutting her off as Lady Kensington began to smile, her eyes flashing with a darkness that Jeffery had not seen before. "Good evening, Lady Kensington." He turned on his heel and strode away from her, hearing her quiet, tinkling laugh chasing after him, adding to his misery as he stumbled forward, further into the shadows and further away from her. He hated himself for having to agree, for having to do all that she demanded without hesitation, yet he knew that she would do all that she had threatened—and more—if he did not.

"Goodness, you look as though..." Lord Swinton began to chuckle, only to trail off, his smile fading as he took in Jeffery's appearance. "I see Lady Kensington has spoken to you."

"You knew she would be here this evening?" Jeffery grated as Lord Swinton nodded. "I did not."

Lord Swinton studied him for a moment. "What has she asked of you?"

"I am to find a gentleman named Lord Bellingham. I am to give him specific instructions. Thereafter, I am to hand him a locket of some description and then inform Lady Kensington that it has been done."

Lord Swinton's brows rose. "You are to speak to Lady Kensington directly?" he repeated as Jeffery nodded slowly, rubbing one hand over his face in frustration. "And quite how are you to do so without everyone in the *ton* being aware of it?"

"I do not know," Jeffery replied heavily. "But she was most insistent."

"Because it will look to the *beau monde* as though you

have approached her rather than the truth," Lord Swinton murmured, shaking his head. "She is a manipulative creature, I think."

There were harsher words in Jeffery's head than that, but he did not allow them to be spoken. Instead, he let out a long breath and dropped his hand back to his side. "There is no other choice but to do as she asks," he said heavily. "I have no knowledge of this 'Lord Bellingham,' but evidently, he is here this evening."

"I believe I know him," Lord Swinton said slowly. "He is not at all enamored with society, however, and is, in fact, very quiet and dull by all accounts. I am surprised that Lady Kensington has sought him out, given that she usually chases gentlemen who, at the very least, have an interesting character!"

"Ours is not to reason why," Jeffery quipped before turning to face the crowd a little more. His stomach twisted as he remembered what Lady Kensington had said. "It appears that Lady Kensington has introduced herself to Lady Rebecca," he told his friend, seeing the widening of Lord Swinton's eyes and nodding gravely. "I do not know what I am to do, but I certainly do not like the thought of such an acquaintance."

"Speaking of the lady..." Lord Swinton gestured just a little ahead of them, where Jeffery spotted Lady Rebecca dancing with another gentleman, her steps sure and certain. She was, he considered, the most elegant of dancers, a gentle smile on her face as she continued through the dance. A sigh slipped from his mouth as he realized it was a pleasure he would not be able to enjoy for some time, given that his reputation was still very much being questioned.

"You think very well of her."

"I do," Jeffery replied without hesitation. "There is no shame in that, I think. She is quite extraordinary, given that she has shown so much judgment and refuses to be pulled into the gossip of the *ton*. She does not believe what is said without question, refuses to accept something as truth when it might well not be so." Glancing at Lord Swinton, he gave a small, wry smile. "I cannot help but think well of her. I cannot help but want to improve my acquaintance with her, even though I believe it would be best for her to remain far from me."

Lord Swinton chuckled. "I doubt you would be able to do so, even if you wished to," he replied as the dance came to a close. "Lady Rebecca has a firmness of mind and a sureness of spirit that I believe even you would not be able to stand against."

Jeffery made to say more, only for Lady Rebecca's eyes to alight on his, her lips instantly curving into a smile as she curtsied towards her partner, thanking him for the dance. Feeling the quickened beat of his heart, the awareness of his desire to draw close to her, Jeffery dropped his head and looked away, not wanting anyone in the ballroom to notice their connection.

"Might I ask," Lord Swinton said slowly, clearly aware of all that Jeffery felt at present. "If you were not in such difficulties, would you consider courting Lady Rebecca?"

The answer came to Jeffery's lips in an instant and without a modicum of hesitation. "Of course, I would do so," he said. "I think her the most extraordinary lady. She is beautiful, wise in her considerations, intelligent in her speech, and, as you have said, quite determined." Yet, even as he spoke, sorrow thrust through his heart, and he sighed heavily. "But it cannot be so, as you know."

"Do not give up hope," Lord Swinton replied calmly. "It may yet come to pass."

"How could it ever occur?" Jeffery retorted, shaking his head. "Lord Kensington and Lady Kensington remain in society, yes, but Lady Kensington is now considered poorly in the eyes of the *ton*. I am caught up in that scandal, even though I have done nothing wrong. The duke would never consider me, given my reputation. It is quite impossible."

Lord Swinton considered for a moment. "But if Lord Kensington were to admit that he knew full well you had not behaved improperly, then—"

"He will not do so," Jeffery answered with a shake of his head. "It is an impossibility, Swinton, and I will not entertain it. Not when such hopes are quite foolish indeed."

There was no opportunity to say more, however, for in the next moment, the very person they had been discussing was before them, with Lady Hayward, Lady Anna, and Lady Selina joining them. Lady Selina and Lady Anna immediately began to discuss something with Lord Swinton, something they had spoken of during the afternoon call, whilst Jeffery was left with Lady Rebecca and Lady Hayward's company.

"Good evening," he murmured, finding himself quite unable to remove his gaze from Lady Rebecca. She was all the more beautiful this evening, her red curls burning bronze in the candlelight. Her cheeks were a little pink from the exertion of dancing, her eyes warm and her smile seeming to soothe his own pains without her even being aware of it.

"We had a most unpleasant encounter, Lord Richmond." Lady Hayward's sharp voice took away some of Jeffery's pleasure in seeing Lady Rebecca again, and he was forced to return his gaze to Lady Hayward, his smile dropping from his face as he took in the dismay on hers.

"Indeed," he remarked as Lady Rebecca dropped her head. "Might I ask with whom?"

"With Lady Kensington," came the reply. She studied him for some moments, leaving Jeffery wondering if Lady Hayward was about to criticize him in some way, to ask him if he knew anything about this particular encounter, only for Lady Hayward to sigh heavily and drop her gaze for a moment.

"I was wrong to judge you so harshly the first time we met," she said, eventually lifting her gaze to his and giving him a small smile. "Lady Kensington is much worse in her character than I had ever expected, and, for my lack of judgment in this matter, I apologize." She bobbed a quick curtsy before lifting her chin again to look up at him steadily. "I was persuaded by the whispers of gossip I overheard. But it seems that Lady Rebecca's judgment in this was quite correct."

"Please." Jeffery held out one hand, a small smile on his face. "There is no need to explain, Lady Hayward. You were doing your best for your charge, and I could never hold that against you."

Lady Hayward smiled back at him, a look of relief on her face. "You are most generous, Lord Richmond," she said before turning to join the other conversation with Lord Swinton.

Jeffery turned his gaze towards Lady Rebecca, finding that the tight band that had formed across his chest when Lady Hayward had first spoken immediately beginning to loosen.

"How are you this evening, Lord Richmond?" Lady Rebecca asked, her expression gentle. "It seems that we are not to have the pleasure of dancing after all." She held up her dance card and gave him a rueful smile. "It seems that Lady Hayward's intention to introduce me to as many gentlemen of the *ton* as possible has succeeded."

He tried to laugh, but the sound stuck in his throat, for something within him began to worry that she might then discover another gentleman to take interest in. Why was it that he felt such a thing when he had only just told Lord Swinton that he would not be able to encourage anything further between himself and Lady Rebecca? He knew he could not do so. In fact, he was foolish just to think of it—but the thought would not leave him.

"Perhaps another opportunity will present itself," he found himself saying as Lady Rebecca's smile grew. "I should very much like it if there was to be such an opportunity, Lady Rebecca."

"As would I, Lord Richmond," she replied, a little breathlessly. "I am very glad that you have been happy to welcome me into your company, albeit for a short time." Her eyes searched his as her smile remained. "I do hope you are encouraged by it."

"Your company is always encouraging, Lady Rebecca," he said honestly. "It is a brightness pushing aside the dark clouds. It is a beautiful song that chases away my melancholy. All in all, Lady Rebecca, your company and your willingness to seek my company for yourself has been a great encouragement to me, and one that I do not think I could do without."

He had said a great deal, he realized, seeing the gentle pink that rushed to her cheeks as she held his gaze. He had spoken openly, had told her of his heart, and had found a way to express all that he felt without hesitation. And yet it had been words of great meaning, that told her she was of such importance to him that he did not know how he would be able to continue on within society without her.

Jeffery swallowed hard. Perhaps he had said too much.

"Do you truly feel such a way, Lord Richmond?"

He could not deny it now. He could not take back what he had said and pretend it was not so. She was asking him to speak the truth, to confirm to her what he had said, and the opportunity was now before him to do precisely that. What the consequences would be of such truths, he did not know, and part of him did not want to take the risk of speaking when he could not be sure of what would happen next.

But his heart yearned to do so. The desire to tell her all that he felt at present was within him, burning up slowly until he felt as though he had no other choice.

"Lady Rebecca," he said quietly, praying that Lady Hayward would not overhear him. "I have struggled with wanting your company and seeking to protect you. You have fought against the latter, although I cannot yet entirely understand your reasons for doing so." He saw her lips quirk, and a smile caught his own. "I have found myself so enamored that even to think of you has brought a hope to my heart that lifts it from the pain and confusion and doubt that continue to surround me." Spreading his hands, he closed his eyes momentarily. "I wish I could rid myself of this poor reputation, Lady Rebecca. Perhaps then I might have been able to follow the wishes of my heart."

For a few moments, Lady Rebecca said nothing. Her gaze was gentle, her expression warm, and, much to his astonishment, she held out her hand to him in the boldest manner.

Jeffery hesitated for a moment, then took it in his, bowing over it as any gentleman might. The urge to brush his lips against her gloved hand was intense, but he did not permit himself to do so, knowing that Lady Hayward would be all too aware of his action.

When he lowered her hand, however, Lady Rebecca did not release his grip. Instead, she held his hand tightly for a few moments, saying nothing but with such a look in her eyes that Jeffery felt his breath catch in his chest.

"Permit me to speak to my father, Lord Richmond," she said eventually, her words so faint that he struggled to hear them. "Allow me to discover whether or not he would permit your court."

Jeffery shook his head and immediately saw the disappointment flare in her eyes. "It would do no good,

Lady Rebecca," he said gently. "Your father is a duke. I am a disgraced Marquess."

"But perhaps I can convince him of—"

"Unless there is a way I can prove my innocence, then there is nothing that can be done," he told her kindly. "If you choose to speak to the duke, then I cannot prevent you, but I fear then that he would only force you away from my company entirely. And that, Lady Rebecca, would bring me a great deal of pain."

Lady Rebecca sighed and let go of his hand. "Then mayhap we can find a way to prove you are not guilty of what is spoken about you," she said as Lady Hayward turned back to them, making it clear by her presence that their time for conversation was at an end. "I will not give up, Lord Richmond."

This made him smile and, whilst he regretted that she had to depart from his company, he felt so blessed by the company he had enjoyed that his heart was filled with a contentment that buoyed his spirits.

"I did not think you would, Lady Rebecca," he replied, inclining his head and catching her bright smile before she was led away by Lady Hayward, her sisters following in her wake. A sigh of pleasure left him as he watched her depart, realizing he had forgotten all about Lady Kensington and her demands.

"It appears you had an excellent conversation with Lady Rebecca, Richmond."

Jeffery looked at his friend. "I would court her if I could," he found himself saying, remembering just how fast his heart had beat when he had taken her hand in his.

"I do not think I have ever met anyone like her before. She is extraordinary."

"And the fact that she continues to seek you out also speaks of her ongoing interest," Lord Swinton commented as Jeffery nodded. "If you could find a way to court her, to even consider matrimony, then—"

"I have told her I cannot, not unless I am able to prove myself entirely innocent of all that Lady Kensington had said of me," Jeffery interrupted firmly. He turned to his friend, who had an exasperated look on his face. "Could you imagine the daughter of a duke being wed to someone who has a stain on his reputation? Who has been called a rogue and a scoundrel?" Shaking his head, his lips twisted in frustration. "The whispers would only multiply, Swinton. They would chase after her as well as after me. She would hear, many times over, that I am surely not a faithful husband, that I would, in time, pursue others rather than remain with her. She might not believe them, of course, but such rumors would only injure her heart, and it could be years before such things are gone from society." Rubbing one hand over his eyes, he looked back at his friend. "And if I am blessed with offspring, what if they return to London and hear of my supposed misdemeanors? Someone will say, 'that is the son or daughter of Lord Richmond, who was a great scoundrel back when he was courting Lady Richmond,' and then what are my children to think of me? Will they believe what I have to say or will they begin to question what they know of me?"

"You are thinking much too far ahead," Lord Swinton protested weakly, betraying his awareness that such things were all as Jeffery had suggested. "Surely you cannot…" He sighed and looked away. "Yes, I can see what you are saying." His head lifted and sighed again. "Lady Rebecca is aware of it also, I suppose."

"She is," Jeffery admitted with a wry smile, "although she is quite determined that we should find a way to remove these rumors entirely."

"And just how are we to go about such a thing?" Lord Swinton asked as Jeffery allowed himself to laugh. "Does she have any pertinent suggestions?"

Jeffery shook his head. "Neither of us has any thought on the matter at all, I am afraid. But that does not mean that we should throw our hands up and declare that we are quite at a loss!"

Lord Swinton grinned. "Not when there is such a thing as your happiness with Lady Rebecca to be secured, Richmond," he agreed, slapping Jeffery on the shoulder. "Then let us begin to explore what is at hand so we can overcome this difficulty."

The smile on Jeffery's face faltered as he suddenly recalled the locket that he had been given and Lady Kensington's demand. "That must come after I have done as Lady Kensington requests," he said slowly as Lord Swinton began to frown, his grin gone in an instant. His happiness slipped away as he pulled the locket out and held it in his hand. "I forgot for a short time that she still has this tight hold upon me." His eyes lifted back to Lord Swinton, who was frowning hard. "And quite how I am to free myself from her, I do not yet know."

CHAPTER TEN

"Speaking to your father will do no good, Lady Rebecca."

It had been ten days since Rebecca had heard Lord Richmond speak with such warmth and fondness, ten days since she had decided, within her own heart, that she would find a way for their acquaintance to move a little further. To know that he wanted to court her, that the desire to do so was within him, had brought such a joy to her spirit that she had felt herself almost renewed. Of course, Lady Hayward was well aware of the situation as it now stood, for Rebecca had been honest with her about what Lord Richmond had said, as well as her own growing feelings for the gentleman. These last ten days, they had spent time conversing together, whether in a quiet bookshop where they had met or over afternoon tea at Lady Hayward's residence. The duke, of course, would not have permitted the gentleman entry, had he known, and yet Rebecca felt herself growing all the more eager to tell her father the truth.

"He will not accept Lord Richmond, Lady Rebecca," Lady Hayward continued as they walked into the rooms that had been hired by Lord Greymark for his evening assembly, with Lady Anna and Lady Selina behind them. "You know he will not."

Rebecca sighed and nodded. She had been trying to convince herself that her father would be willing to consider what she had to say, should she try to explain how she believed that Lord Richmond was innocent of the rumors that swirled about him. The duke was not the sort of man to listen carefully and to consider whatever Rebecca said. Rather, he would have already made up his mind and could not permit Rebecca even to speak of the gentleman! What Lord Richmond had said had been quite correct; it had only been her fervor that had made her eager to talk to her father.

"He will be here this evening," she told Lady Hayward, who nodded, although one brow lifted. "I am sure he will be present."

"I just wish I could have found you a gentleman that was without any difficulties at all," Lady Hayward replied with a sigh. "Although I confess that I was the one who encouraged you to find a gentleman that captured your heart. It appears that Lord Richmond has been the one to do so!"

"It is something that I have been entirely unable to prevent," Rebecca replied honestly. "If only I could think of a way for Lord Richmond to…" She trailed off, shaking her head. "Lord Kensington is the only one able to refute such rumors. I highly doubt he would be willing to do so."

"As would I," Lady Hayward replied, pressing Rebecca's arm in consolation. "But do not give up hope as yet, Lady Rebecca. There might yet be a way."

"I thank you," Rebecca answered, truly appreciative. "I always believed I would wed a gentleman out of nothing more than sheer practicality. However, you showed me an entirely different way of thinking, and I am truly grateful to you for it."

Lady Hayward laughed. "Even though it has caused us both a good deal of difficulty?"

Rebecca could not help but chuckle. "Yes, even then, Lady Hayward," she answered with a smile. "I am very grateful, indeed."

⁓

THE EVENING HAD GONE VERY WELL THUS far, but Rebecca had not seen any sign of Lord Richmond and had to confess that she was somewhat disappointed. He had said he would be here this evening and yet appeared to be either absent or delayed. Lord Swinton was present, of course, and whilst he had greeted her and engaged both her and her two sisters for a dance each, he had not made mention of Lord Richmond. When Rebecca had asked him if he knew where Lord Richmond was this evening, he had shaken his head and apologized that, no, he did not know. However, the way that he had not looked into her eyes made Rebecca wonder as to whether or not he spoke the truth.

"You are not enjoying the dance, Lady Rebecca?"

Rebecca gave herself a slight shake, realizing that she

had been distracted in her dance with Lord Swinton and giving him an apologetic smile.

"Forgive me, Lord Swinton," she said, her words stalling for a moment as they moved away from each other in the dance before coming back together again. "It is only that I am concentrating hard on making quite certain not to make a mistake!"

This seemed to appease Lord Swinton, for he smiled and nodded feverishly as though he wanted to both sympathize and encourage.

"But of course," he said as she stepped away again, ready to be turned by another gentleman. "I quite understand."

Rebecca made to reply, only to be suddenly pulled back as something tugged at the bottom of her skirts. With a cry, she stumbled back and practically fell into the gentleman behind her—the gentleman who had accidentally trodden on the back of her gown. An ominous sound of ripping caught her ears, and she cried out again as the gentleman caught her and helped her back to her feet, apologizing profusely for his mistake. Rebecca regained her composure as quickly as she could, her face rather pink with both embarrassment and the exertion of dancing.

"Lady Rebecca!" Lord Swinton was beside her in a moment, their dancing set quite ruined now by what had occurred. "Let me escort you back at once to Lady Hayward."

Much to her relief, the music came to a close, and the remaining dance sets thanked their partners and began to step away from the floor. Taking Lord Swinton's proffered arm, she made her way back to Lady Hayward, who was now watching her anxiously.

"I am quite all right," Rebecca said quickly as Lady Hayward reached for her. "Another gentleman has torn my hem, however."

Lady Hayward did not even look at the gown, however, quickly thanking Lord Swinton, who took his leave as though he were the one who would be blamed for such an accident. Rebecca thanked him and then turned back to Lady Hayward, a wry smile on her face.

"I must hope there is a parlor of sorts that can help with this," she said as Lady Hayward nodded.

"There is, my dear," she said, although her eyes darted back towards the dance floor. "My lady's maid is there. Although your sisters have only just left my side to dance the cotillion." Her brow furrowed. "Might you wait?"

"I am sure I can make my way there and then return to you," Rebecca replied, not wanting to linger with her embarrassment of having her gown ripped and torn. "It is not far?"

Lady Hayward hesitated, looking from Rebecca to her sisters and then back again. "It is just there," she said eventually, indicating a door that was only a short distance from Rebecca. "That door leads you to a hallway, and to your immediate right is the correct door." She bit her lip. "I will have a footman accompany you, I think. You will return at once?" Beckoning to a nearby footman, she quickly explained what she required him to do.

"Of course," Rebecca promised, following after the footman and quickly hurrying through the guests and towards the small parlor. Pushing open the door, she was relieved to find Lady Hayward's lady's maid coming towards her at once. Indicating the rip to her gown, Rebecca sank down into a waiting chair and let the maid take care of her gown.

∽

"There you go, miss."

Rebecca looked down at her gown with both satisfaction and relief, glad that the maid had been able to assist her. "Well done," she said, barely able to see where the rip had been and noting how a blush came into the lady's cheeks as she stood with her hands clasped tightly in front of her and a small smile on her face. "You have done very well. I will make certain to tell Lady Hayward of your hard work."

"Thank you, my lady," the maid replied, leaving Rebecca free to rise to her feet and make her way from the room. Stepping back into the hallway, she saw the footman waiting for her, his back towards her as he looked out at the guests. Rebecca was about to make him aware of her presence, only for something to catch her attention.

She could not quite say what it was—a sound, perhaps, a creak or a whisper—but whatever it was, Rebecca turned her head and frowned. The sound came again, a quiet laugh that echoed down the hallway towards her, and, instantly, Rebecca knew she should not linger. She ought to tell the footman she was ready to return, ought to inform him that she needed to go back at once to Lady Hayward. After all, had she not promised that she would do so? Her heart quickened within her as she heard a low rumble of a voice come down towards her, her cheeks heating furiously as she lingered, unable to explain why she stayed so.

"Come now, Richmond."

The words were a little clearer now, and Rebecca stiffened, her whole body frozen in place, her mouth a little ajar from where she had been going to speak to the footman. Lord Richmond was behind her? And just whom was he with?

Her heart still pounding furiously in her chest, Rebecca turned on her heel and began to make her way up the hallway. She knew very well that she was not doing as Lady Hayward had asked, knew she should return at once, but the mention of Lord Richmond's name had thrown all sense from her. The door behind her opened, admitting a few ladies into the hallway who all went into the small parlor, their voice echoing up towards her and permitting Rebecca to hurry forward without her footsteps being overheard. The hallway split to the right and to the left, and Rebecca slowed her steps, not certain where she ought to go.

And then she heard the voice again.

"Lady Kensington, I have done all that you asked."

Her eyes closed, and Rebecca pressed herself against the wall, fear and dread clutching at her heart.

"I know, but there is still more that must be done," she heard Lady Kensington say, her voice dripping with honey. "You cannot turn away from me now, not after all you have done for my sake."

Rebecca shuddered, not wanting to think about what such a thing might mean. Lord Richmond had told her he was free of guilt, that he had not done as the *ton* whispered, but was she wrong to believe him? From what she heard, it seemed that she had been quite mistaken. Turning blindly, she hurried down the hallway and back towards the footman, tears beginning to blind her vision.

"Take me back," she whispered, the footman turning around quickly, evidently surprised she was there. "Take me to Lady Hayward at once."

The footman nodded and made to step forward, only for Rebecca to hear someone calling her name.

"Lady Rebecca?"

She half-turned, only to shake her head and gesture for the footman to step forward.

"Lady Rebecca, please!"

Recognizing Lord Richmond's voice, Rebecca blinked back her tears and turned around and looked at him, keeping her head high and her chin lifted.

"Lord Richmond," she said, aware of the tremor in her voice. "I thought you absent this evening." Her eyes narrowed just a fraction. "But it seems you were otherwise engaged." Her throat began to ache as she held his gaze, seeing how he looked at her with wide eyes, perhaps only now realizing that she had overheard something. They stood there for a long moment, with neither one of them saying a word. Tears began to flood back into Rebecca's eyes, and she blinked them back with effort.

"Lady Rebecca, I—"

Behind him, Rebecca suddenly saw Lady Kensington emerge from around the corner of the hallway, moving forward slowly towards them. As she drew nearer, Rebecca saw that there was a small, cruel smile cross her face. Her stomach dropped, her heart twisted painfully, and she turned away from Lord Richmond, no longer able to look at him.

"Please, Lady Rebecca!"

His hand caught hers, but she did not even look back at him. Instead, she wrenched away and walked back towards the footman, who quickly led her towards Lady Hayward. Rebecca did not look back, her heart aching and her eyes burning with tears. She had been wrong. She had been entirely mistaken. Lord Richmond was not who she believed him to be, was not the sort of gentleman she ought to have given her heart to. Lady Hayward had been correct to pull her away from him, and yet she had been the one to insist upon it.

Little wonder that Lord Swinton would not look at me earlier when I asked him about Lord Richmond's presence, she thought to herself as the footman presented her back to Lady Hayward, who was now standing with Lady Anna and Lady Selina. *He must have known that he was with Lady Kensington.*

"Your gown looks quite perfect," Lady Hayward said with delight as Rebecca blinked rapidly, trying to recall why she had left Lady Hayward's company in the first place. "My maid has done very well."

"Yes, yes," Rebecca murmured, her mind feeling dull and heavy as she saw Lady Hayward frown. "I said I would inform you that she had done such an excellent fix, Lady Hayward. I am very pleased with it."

"Lady Anna?"

A gentleman came to join Lady Anna, bowing and requesting her hand for this dance. Another came for Lady Selina, and Lady Hayward smiled and nodded, gesturing for them to take their places on the floor.

"You are not engaged for this dance, Lady Rebecca?" Lady Hayward asked as Rebecca looked back at her, her thoughts still muddled and her heart still painful. "Your card?"

It took a moment for Rebecca to lift her arm and pick up her dance card. "No," she said, a little relieved that she would not have to pretend that all was well to another gentleman. "No, I am not."

Lady Hayward stepped closer and put her hand on Rebecca's arm. "Lady Rebecca, what is wrong?" she asked gently, looking into Rebecca's face. "Something has happened, has it not?"

A single tear fell from Rebecca's eye, and she brushed it away quickly, not wanting Lady Hayward to see it—but it was much too late.

"Oh, my dear," Lady Hayward said softly. "Might you be able to keep your composure until this dance is completed? We can return to your father's house at once."

Rebecca shook her head, knowing just how disappointed her sisters would be. "There is no need," she said hoarsely. "I will be myself in a moment."

Lady Hayward eyes continued to search Rebecca's face. "I do not think you will be recovered in a moment," she said gently. "But if you wish to stay, then I cannot prevent you. Although I do think we should return home if you are upset, Lady Rebecca. To remain here could bring difficulties with it."

"You speak of the *ton*," Rebecca said, dropping her head and forcing her tears back with an effort. "You think they will notice my upset."

With a small nod, Lady Hayward took in a deep breath and let go of Rebecca 's arm. "Your sisters will understand, Lady Rebecca. The gentlemen on your card will accept the notion that you have a headache or some such thing. There is truly no need to remain."

But Rebecca shook her head again, quite determined that she would remain. Lord Richmond would not chase her from this place, would not be able to see her hurrying from the assembly because of his actions. No, rather, he would see her dancing and enjoying the remainder of the evening, even though it would be nothing other than a pretense.

"It is Lord Richmond," she said, managing to speak without too much difficulty. "I saw—overheard him speaking with Lady..." She could not speak her name. "Lady..."

"I know who you refer to," Lady Hayward interrupted, her face now tight with anger that Rebecca had not expected. "Then it appears that he is not as we both believed."

Rebecca swallowed hard and looked away, feeling the ache return to her throat as she fought desperately to keep herself entirely composed. "It appears so, Lady Hayward."

The lady closed her eyes and let out a long, slow breath. "Then it is little wonder you are upset," she said softly. "My dear Lady Rebecca, I am truly sorry to hear such news. Are you sure you will not return home?"

Taking in a steadying breath, Rebecca set her shoulders and nodded. "I will remain," she said with as much firmness as she could. "And from this moment shall do my utmost to forget entirely about the Marquess of Richmond."

Lady Hayward made to say something, only for Lord Swinton to suddenly appear, bowing his head before he fixed his gaze to her face.

"Lady Rebecca," he said hastily as Lady Hayward began to frown. "There is something I must tell you. Something that Lord Richmond has kept from you."

"With all due respect, Lord Swinton, now is not the time to be speaking to Lady Rebecca of Lord Richmond," Lady Hayward interrupted, but Lord Swinton shook his head, his jaw working for a moment. Rebecca did not know what to think, a little surprised at the fervent look in his eyes.

"It is not as you think, Lady Rebecca," he said urgently. "Please. Just spare me a moment of your time and I will explain all."

Rebecca took in a deep breath and saw Lady Hayward's dark frown, aware that everything in her wanted to refuse, wanted to tell Lord Swinton that she did not want to know anything more about him. But a tiny flicker of hope ignited in her heart, and, despite herself, she gave him a small nod.

"Go on, Lord Swinton," she said, her voice a little hoarse. "Say what you must, but do not expect me to believe it."

Lord Swinton's relief was palpable. "Thank you, Lady Rebecca," he said quietly. "I hope that, by the time I have finished, you will find yourself considering Lord Richmond in an entirely new light. In fact, I am quite certain of it."

CHAPTER ELEVEN

A shudder ran through Jeffery as he saw Lady Rebecca hurrying from him. Lady Kensington had demanded his company almost the moment he had arrived, showing her husband a small hole in her gown that she had to have repaired almost at once. Without any other choice, Jeffery had made his way after her, only to hear yet more demands of his time and the efforts that had filled him with such anger, it had burned at his heart.

Only for him to hear footsteps scurrying away from where he and Lady Kensington stood. His eyes had caught sight of a lady with red curls tumbling down her back as she hurried back towards the door, and in his heart, Jeffery knew who it was.

Lady Rebecca.

"What a shame!" Lady Kensington exclaimed, sounding quite distraught even though Jeffery knew that such sentiment was entirely devoid of her character. "Although it seems as though I will no longer be able to hold her over you as a threat." A small smile curled about her lips. "Even though I can tell that you care for her."

Jeffery could not reply to her, his words sticking in his throat as he saw Lady Rebecca hurry back into the crowd. He wanted to explain, wanted to have the opportunity to tell her what had been discussed between himself and Lady Kensington, but knew she would not accept him. He had seen the look in her eyes, had seen the pain ripple across her face as he had caught her hand. There was no simple way to tell her the truth about it.

"That does not matter, however," Lady Kensington cooed, turning around to face him and ignoring the other ladies who were coming in and out from the small parlor to his left. "You have only one more thing to do for me, and then it shall all be at an end!"

"I will do nothing more for you," Jeffery bit out, his eyes slowly traveling towards Lady Kensington's face and finding that his anger was burning with such fury that it was difficult for him to contain it. "You have done enough, Lady Kensington."

"I have done very little!" she protested, smiling at him as though they were great friends. "You have been *very* willing thus far, Lord Richmond, and such willingness must continue. There is, as I have said, only one small matter remaining. And I will inform you of it tomorrow morning, by letter."

"I will not read it."

"You will." Leaning a little closer, she set her cold, hard gaze to his. "Just because Lady Rebecca has seen us conversing does not mean that I cannot have her thrown from society for good. Do you really wish to allow that to happen?"

Jeffery dropped his head, his resistance gone. Lady Kensington laughed softly, clearly aware of her victory. She reached out and squeezed his hand before making her way into the parlor herself without so much as a glance back towards him. Jeffery remained precisely where he was, his whole body tight with fury, his anger burning hotter than it had ever done before, although his heart pounded and ached with pain. He wanted to rush in after Lady Kensington, to grasp her arms and shake her until she realized that he was not going to go about her bidding any longer.

But he could not.

There was one last thing for him to do. One last request that Lady Kensington was to put to him. And then, it seemed, it would be at an end. He could not quite understand why it would be so, what had changed for her to decide that he would be free of her grip on his life, but Jeffery did not care. It was too late. Lady Rebecca had already seen him conversing with Lady Kensington and had come to the worst possible conclusion.

And yet, he would protect her. He would do as Lady Kensington asked without hesitation so she would not injure Lady Rebecca in any way.

Lifting his head, Jeffery followed after Lady Rebecca back into the hubbub of guests, although, by now, he had very little idea where she had gone. His shoulders slumped as he meandered forward, not looking to the right or left but making his way through the crowd, a broken man. It was time for him to leave this place, time for him to return home where he might nurse his broken spirit in peace.

"Richmond!"

Lord Swinton's bright voice was nothing more than a fresh agony to Jeffery's soul.

"Where have you been?" Lord Swinton exclaimed loudly, his face a little red from dancing. "I have danced every dance thus far, and I am sure that there would be some here willing to dance with you also, if you would wish it?"

Jeffery lifted his head and looked at his friend, seeing how his smile began to fade away at Jeffery's expression.

"I am returning home," Jeffery said heavily. "And then, once tomorrow comes and the responsibility towards Lady Kensington comes to an end, I will make my way back to my estate."

Lord Swinton blinked in surprise. "Your estate?" he repeated, all the more astonished. "Why ever should you do so?"

Jeffery shook his head and raked one hand through his hair, his spirits lower than ever before. "Lady Rebecca came upon Lady Kensington and I conversing," he said, each word seeming to bruise his lips as he spoke. "There is nothing left for me here. It is all at an end."

Lord Swinton made to stop him, but Jeffery ignored him entirely, walking on towards the door, desperate to escape. Once outside, the darkness of the night wrapped him in a shroud and added its heavy weight to his soul, leaving him feeling weary and entirely broken. There was not even a single modicum of hope remaining. Everything was at an end, and he would never see Lady Rebecca again.

~

"You will write to Lord Bellingham, meet with him, and will give him the box you purchased from Sturrock and Sons as well as the other items that you have kept in your care. He is expecting you to do so. Thereafter, you will write a short note to me and inform me that all has been done as you intended."

The note from Lady Kensington made very little sense to Jeffery, but given that he had no hope, no flicker of happiness nor murmur of content in his soul, it made very little difference. He would do as he had been asked and then would remove himself back to his estate. Lady Kensington would have no further part in his life. But neither, it seemed, would Lady Rebecca.

The box Lady Kensington had referred to was one he had purchased from Sturrock and Sons. He had been informed some days ago that a small item had been set aside for him and that he was to pay for it and return home. Why now he was to give it to Lord Bellingham—a quiet and staid gentleman that Jeffery had met only once before—he could not even imagine.

Not that such a thing mattered.

With a sigh, Jeffery rose from his study chair and made his way to the window, pressing his hands down on the windowsill as he looked out below him. Nothing in his view was of any interest. Nothing there intrigued him. His spirit was low. His heart was broken. And he felt nothing but regret.

"Richmond!"

Jeffery turned, startled, as Lord Swinton threw back the door and hurried into the room.

"For heaven's sake, man, whatever are you doing here?" he demanded as Jeffery turned slowly back towards the window, having no eagerness to discuss the matter with his friend. "Why are you not at Lady Hayward's? Or at the duke's townhouse, seeking out Lady Rebecca?"

"Do not torment me with such suggestions!" Jeffery rounded on him, his hands curling into tight fists, fury slamming through him all at once. "It is over! It is done! Lady Kensington has achieved her great victory despite my attempts to bring her low."

Lord Swinton stared at him, his mouth agape, before he strode towards Jeffery purposefully, slamming his hands onto either side of Jeffery's arms. "Whatever are you talking of, Richmond?" he said fiercely. "I spoke to Lady Rebecca *and* Lady Hayward last evening. I told them everything. Everything that you had kept from them in the hope of protecting Lady Rebecca from Lady Kensington. Did you not receive my note? And did they not write to you also?"

Jeffery stared at his friend, his eyes widening as he realized what Lord Swinton meant. "I—I received letters this morning," he murmured, his anger beginning to fade away. "I have not yet opened them. My...my torment has been too great."

Lord Swinton dropped his hands. "Lady Rebecca was deeply upset last evening, as you must know," he began. "I could not permit her to continue believing the worst of you. I told her the truth. I begged her to believe me, and, much to my astonishment, Lady Hayward was the one to encourage her to do so." He turned on his heel. "I said you would explain it all to them today also so that she could be thoroughly assured that I had told her the truth."

"Then I must go," Jeffery breathed, his heart beginning to hammer furiously as he realized what Lord Swinton had done. "Thank you, Swinton. I—" He did not know what to say, how to express his thanks to his friend, but Lord Swinton only grinned.

"You care about Lady Rebecca," he said. "I believe she cares for you. I cannot see both of you so sorrowful and troubled without speaking up. But I should suggest that you hurry. The lady will be waiting."

Jeffery nodded, hurrying to his desk and snatching up the letters he had received earlier that day. Flicking through them, he quickly found the one that bore the correct seal and broke it open.

"'My dear Lord Richmond,'" he read aloud, his heart pounding. "'I have been utterly astonished to hear what Lord Swinton has said. Please, if it is true, then call upon me at Lady Hayward's this afternoon. I must hear it from your lips. Yours, Lady Rebecca.'"

Clenching his jaw so that he would not give in to the shattering emotions threatened now to plague him, Jeffery took a few moments to regain his composure before he turned back to his friend.

"Let us depart," he said a little hoarsely. "She is waiting for me at Lady Hayward's."

Lord Swinton nodded. "I have the carriage waiting," he said as Jeffery let out a long breath, setting his shoulders and walking to the door. "We will be there within the hour."

∽

Walking into Lady Hayward's drawing-room felt like some sort of dream. Jeffery had believed that he would never be able to do so again, would never let his gaze settle on Lady Rebecca's beautiful face, and yet both things were occurring at the very same moment.

Lady Rebecca rose to her feet the instant he came into the room, and Jeffery could not take his eyes from her. Her face was a little paler than usual, and her eyes lacked their sparkle, her hands held in front of her, her fingers twisting together.

He wanted desperately to go to her, to take her hands in his and to plead her forgiveness, but he knew he could not. Instead, he bowed towards her and then to Lady Hayward, who was watching him with something of a severe look.

"Thank you for permitting me to call upon you, Lady Rebecca," Jeffery began as he was waved to a chair by Lady Hayward. "I am sorry for the pain and suffering you have endured since last evening. It must have come as a very great shock to you."

"Yes, it did," Lady Rebecca told him without hesitation. "However, from what Lord Swinton has told me, it is not as I believed it to be." Her eyes held his, no flicker of embarrassment in her features as she spoke. "You did not do as the rumors state, and, despite what I heard last evening, you are not continuing a warm acquaintance with Lady Kensington."

"No," Jeffery said quickly, his whole body filled with a determination to prove to her that she was mistaken. "No, I am not, Lady Rebecca. I cannot abide the lady's company, and yet she insists on seeking me out. The reason she does so now is because she wishes me to do something for her, to use me as her pawn simply because she knows that she has the power with which to do so."

Lady Rebecca nodded slowly, glancing towards Lord Swinton, who now looked grave indeed.

"Lord Swinton informed me that it was for my sake that you continued on with Lady Kensington," she said, leaning forward in her chair and looking at Jeffery intently. "Is that true?"

Jeffery nodded, prevented from speaking for a few short minutes as the maids entered with trays laden with refreshments. Jeffery's stomach growled, and he flushed with embarrassment.

"I did not think you would have eaten, Lord Richmond," Lady Hayward explained with a small, knowing smile. "Please, do go on."

Jeffery expressed his thanks quickly but did not reach for anything, wanting instead to finish his explanation. "Lady Kensington warned me that if I did not do as she asked, then there would be consequences," he said quietly. "But they would not be brought down upon my head. Instead, they would touch all those that were in my life. Lord and Lady Merrick, Lord Swinton...and you, Lady Rebecca."

"I told him that there was no great concern when it came to me," Lord Swinton interrupted, gruffly, "and Lord and Lady Merrick were, of course, on their guard, but there was a vulnerability about you, Lady Rebecca, that could not be ignored."

Seeing the frown on Lady Rebecca's face, Jeffery quickly tried to explain. "Lord and Lady Merrick are already wed, and, as such, whilst scandal might attempt to shame them, they felt quite sure they would be able to endure it. Lord Swinton here said the same, although I confess that, having borne the brunt of society's dislike, I am not as certain as he that such a thing would be as easy as he believes it to be." A wry smile touched his lips as he glanced at his friend before returning his gaze to Lady Rebecca. "As for you, Lady Rebecca, you could have become a pariah in society in a moment. The rumors would affect you and your sisters. Your father's good name would be tarnished. I—I could not let such a thing happen, not for my sake."

"And so you did whatever it was that Lady Kensington demanded of you," Lady Hayward interrupted as Jeffery nodded. "To ensure that Lady Rebecca was protected."

Tears began to shimmer in Lady Rebecca's eyes, and Jeffery felt his heart tear, his brow furrowing as he watched her. He wanted to say more, wanted to apologize for pulling her into such a situation, but found that his lips would not move. There appeared to be nothing more to say.

"You could have spoken to me of it, Lord Richmond," Lady Rebecca whispered, one hand now pressed to her heart. "You could have told me the truth of Lady Kensington."

He shook his head. "I was doing all I could to protect you," he replied by way of explanation. "You had already risked a great deal even in acquainting yourself with me, Lady Rebecca. I could not add to your burden."

Silence ran around the room as they sat quietly for some minutes, allowing what had been said to fall into their hearts. Lady Rebecca quickly regained her composure, the tears gone from her eyes as she looked back at Jeffery, her lips still flat and no smile brightening her expression.

"I am sorry," Jeffery found himself saying, the silence became too much for him to bear. "I did not mean to harm you, Lady Rebecca. Nor bring you any great distress. And yet, it seems I have done so."

"Inadvertently," Lady Hayward added firmly. "I can see what you were attempting to do, Lord Richmond, and whilst I will not condone it, I will say that I understand your reasons for it." She leaned forward and poured some tea before gesturing behind her. "There is brandy if you would prefer it to tea."

Lord Swinton rose in an instant, making Lady Rebecca smile. Jeffery felt his heart lift just a little, daring to hope that all would be restored between them, before he accepted a glass from Lord Swinton and, finally, reached for something to eat.

"Might I ask, Lord Richmond," Lady Rebecca began

once they had all taken a few minutes to eat, "what it is that Lady Kensington has been having you do?"

Jeffery frowned. "I should not like to speak of her too much, Lady Rebecca, but if you are insistent upon it, then I will tell you all."

"I think it would be interesting to know," Lady Hayward interjected. "There must be a purpose in her doing such a thing."

Jeffery shrugged one shoulder. "I have always thought that her purpose was to humiliate me," he told her. "She stated that she blames me entirely for what occurred the night Lord Kensington discovered her, for evidently, he has refused to allow her from his sight, although, of course, she has found means to escape from him." A sigh left him. "A punishment of sorts, I suppose."

Lady Rebecca sipped her tea thoughtfully and then set down her teacup. "What have you been required to do?"

A knot of unease tied itself in his stomach, but Jeffery continued on, determinedly. "Initially, it was of very little importance, it seemed. First, I was to give Lord Bellingham instructions—and an item from Lady Kensington herself—so that he would meet with her when her husband was absent. Thereafter, every instruction I was given meant very little to me. I was to visit a particular shop at a particular time and make certain to greet a gentleman present there. I was to inform her which gentleman I had greeted, however."

"Why?" Lady Hayward asked, but Jeffery could only shrug.

"I do not know," he said honestly. "I believe it was so

she might ensure I had done as she asked." He shook his head in frustration. "Of course, I thought nothing of it at first, but every time I did as she bade me, Lord Kensington was present also. It felt as though she was deliberately humiliating me by placing me in the vicinity of the gentleman who believed me to have taken liberties with his wife."

"But you had to do as she asked?"

Jeffery spread his hands. "I had to protect you, Lady Rebecca. As well as the others in my acquaintance. Yes, I did as she asked, even though I hated every moment of it."

"And that is all?" Lady Hayward asked, sounding confused. "You have simply been in a certain place at a certain time?"

Shaking his head, Jeffery reached for his brandy glass. "Recently, I have had to purchase one or two items," he said slowly. "I have never known what these items are, but they have been waiting for me in the shop she directs me to. This last one was from Sturrock and Sons, and I am to meet with Lord Bellingham and give the item to him."

Another murmur of quiet ran around the room.

"How very odd," Lady Hayward said slowly. "And you are certain that you do not know what it was you have purchased?"

"I have only been asked to do so thus far on two occasions," he told her. "The first was at another establishment. I had to collect and pay for two items, although both were very well wrapped and then placed inside a small box. The second is a very small parcel indeed, but, again, has been very well wrapped."

"And you have not thought to unwrap and look inside?"

Jeffery hesitated, then shook his head. "I had thought to do so but fearing that Lady Kensington would be aware of my actions, I chose not to. Besides which," he continued, seeing how Lady Rebecca frowned hard, "it seems that Lady Kensington is quite done with me."

This seemed to bring such a sense of astonishment to the group that for a moment, Jeffery was struck dumb by the immediate response that came from the three of them. All of them began to question him, leaving the air about him seemingly filled with curiosity, confusion, and uncertainty.

"I—I do not know why she has chosen to end the matter, but I am only relieved that she has done so," Jeffery stammered, speaking as loudly as he dared. "Perhaps she has grown weary of me. Mayhap, because of what occurred with you, Lady Rebecca, she realizes that I am less inclined to do as she tells me."

"But that cannot be so," Lord Swinton interrupted. "She knows that you care for Lady Rebecca, and just because she believes that Lady Rebecca is now quite finished with you, Richmond, does not mean that her hold on the situation has changed in any way. She could still easily shame Lady Rebecca within society, just as she has always threatened."

A ripple of unease ran over Jeffery's frame. "That is true enough, I suppose," he said slowly as Lady Rebecca rose to her feet, standing tall in the midst of them all. His eyes rose to hers, seeing a fire burn deep within her eyes, aware of the sudden sense of determination that rose from around her. He felt almost unnerved in her presence, unsure of what she was now to say.

"Then shall we depart?" she asked, astonishing him. "Come, Lord Richmond, there is no time to waste!"

"Time?" he repeated as she nodded fervently, her tea now cooling and forgotten on the small table before her. "Where are we to go, Lady Rebecca?"

She looked at him in surprise as though astonished he had not realized such a thing himself. "Why, we are to return to your townhouse, Lord Richmond," she said, plainly. "We are to look at these parcels and see what is within."

He stared at her for a moment, only to rise to his feet also, seeing Lady Hayward do the same with what appeared to be a very satisfied look on her face. Evidently, she had no real concern over what Lady Rebecca had announced and was quite contented to do as her charge suggested.

"Very well," Jeffery replied as Lady Rebecca smiled at him, her features lighting up. "If you think it will be of benefit, Lady Rebecca."

"I think it will be a great benefit, Lord Richmond," she told him decisively. "You may have been so eager to do all that you can to protect me that you have missed the truth of what Lady Kensington is attempting to do."

This did not make a great deal of sense to him, and he frowned, looking back at her in confusion.

"You mean to say," Lord Swinton interrupted, setting down his now empty brandy glass, "that you believe Lady

Kensington has drawn Lord Richmond into her web and now plans to attack him in some way?"

Lady Rebecca drew in a long breath, lifting her chin as she spoke. "I believe that Lady Kensington is a manipulative, determined lady who will do whatever she can to gain what she desires," she said, her words certain and sure. "And I believe that she *does* intend to punish Lord Richmond for his actions in refusing her advances and having her husband discover her true nature. To state that she now intends to let him free when she could continue as she is at present does not make sense. Unless," she finished, sending a shudder of awareness through Jeffery, "she has gained what it is that she has long desired."

"And what would that be, Lady Rebecca?" Jeffery asked, wishing he had as much insight as she and realizing that she had been correct in what she had said about him being so caught up in his attempts to protect Lady Rebecca that he might well have missed the full picture of what Lady Kensington was attempting to do. "What is it that Lady Kensington wishes for more than anything else?"

Her eyes glowed. "Her freedom," she said slowly. "And that, Lord Richmond, is precisely what I believe you are helping her gain."

CHAPTER TWELVE

Rebecca forced herself to remain calm as she sat in Lord Richmond's carriage, whilst, all the while, she felt as though she were somewhere between exultant joy and despairing tears. She had been through a great deal already, given the difficulties that had come to her last evening, only for her then to awaken this morning with a sense of determination growing within her heart. She had decided to hear it all from Lord Richmond's lips in the hope that everything Lord Swinton had said was true, even though the thought of seeing Lord Richmond again had sent a deep sense of unease all through her. But she had been proven right in her judgments, for Lord Richmond had appeared and explained it all just as Lord Swinton himself had done.

Rebecca had felt her heart begin to heal itself again, had felt her sorrow and pain begin to purge itself from her soul, and in its place came a steady resolve that she would rid Lady Kensington's hold on both her and Lord Richmond's lives. She wanted that freedom, she realized, to know she was entirely free to do as she wished, to act as she pleased, and to consider whomever she wished.

And it had been that thought that had led her to realize just what Lady Kensington wanted.

"I have been foolish, mayhap," Lord Richmond rumbled as the carriage took them back towards his townhouse. "Perhaps I should have opened up these packages. Perhaps I should have discovered immediately what it was I had purchased on her behalf."

"You did not do so, however," Lady Hayward interrupted, "because you were doing all you could to protect those you care for. That is not something to criticize yourself for, Lord Richmond. Rather, it is something that you ought to be commended for."

Rebecca smiled at Lady Hayward's encouraging words, seeing how Lord Richmond looked back at her as their eyes met. There had been such despair in his expression when he had first walked into the room, but now none of that remained. Instead, there was a new light in his eyes, a light that spoke of hope and relief and happiness. Happiness that Rebecca hoped would only grow and expand, so that it might fill both of their hearts together, bringing them close as one.

It did not take long for the carriage to reach Lord Richmond's townhouse, and, hurrying inside, Rebecca was led to Lord Richmond's study—although he apologized profusely for doing so as though they expected him to stand on ceremony and conduct them to the drawing-room where they might take tea together. She laughed and shook her head, telling him that there was no great concern as to where they went and that they only wished to see these particular parcels. Lord Richmond smiled at her, her cheeks a little flushed, before asking them all to sit down whilst he found them.

"And you say that they were already waiting for you?" Lady Hayward asked as Lord Richmond opened up a drawer and took out one box and one small parcel that was wrapped in brown paper and tied with string. "You had to purchase them, however?"

Lord Richmond nodded, biting his lip. "I am to make arrangements with Lord Bellingham and give the items to him," he said slowly. "Although I cannot understand why."

"Most likely because you cannot meet with Lady Kensington and give them to her yourself," Lord Swinton suggested gruffly. "She wants them, whatever they are, and for some reason wishes you to purchase them for her, and, thereafter, to make certain that they reach her hands by giving them to another willing gentleman."

Rebecca wrinkled her nose. "I have conversed with Lord Bellingham," she recalled as Lady Hayward nodded. "I confess that I found him to be…quiet." She frowned. "He said very little and was very difficult to converse with."

"He does not have a strong character," Lady Hayward agreed slowly, "which might make him very easy indeed to manipulate."

Rebecca let out a slow breath and nodded, whilst Lord Richmond frowned, looking down at the two items. She felt her tension rise as he turned his attention to the box, which was also tied with string.

"This was the first I collected and paid for," he said,

trying to undo the knots rather than cut the string itself. "It certainly is a little heavier than the second."

Rebecca watched with growing impatience as his fingers attempted to tug at the knots, making such a hopeless mess of it that she found herself on her feet, walking towards the study table.

"Please, allow me," she said, pulling the box towards her and looking carefully at the knot that had been tied securely. With deft fingers, she tugged at it gently, managing to undo it in a very short space of time. Lord Richmond chuckled as she achieved what he could not, making her look up at him and smile.

"Might you do the same with the other, Lady Rebecca?" he asked, his fingers brushing hers as he reclaimed the box. "I would be grateful for your help."

Heat mounted in her face at his touch, and she quickly picked up the second, smaller parcel and set to work, praying that Lady Hayward did not notice the pink in her cheeks. Lord Richmond undid the string entirely of the box and then, pulling it free, set it aside. Her work completed on the second parcel, she made to step away, but Lord Richmond stayed her hand.

"Might you open it, Lady Rebecca?" he asked quietly. She nodded, swallowing her tension. "I will see what is within this one."

Feeling a little anxious, Rebecca carefully pulled aside the brown paper that wrapped the small parcel. It did not take long, but, once she had revealed the object, there did not come with it a burst of awareness or any sort of understanding. Instead, she studied the small vial, the colorless liquid within, and found herself entirely at a loss.

Lady Hayward was on her feet in a moment, joining Rebecca where she stood, as Lord Swinton made his way towards them also.

"What is it?" Lady Hayward asked as Rebecca shook her head. "Do you know, Lord Swinton? Lord Richmond?"

"I do not," Lord Richmond replied quietly. "But I do know what *this* item is."

Rebecca lifted her eyes from the vial and turned them to the box, a gasp ripping from her throat as she took in the sharp blade that lay there. There was silence for some moments as the four of them studied the knife, tension rising steadily.

"So," Lord Swinton said slowly. "We have a knife and a vial. A vial that I do not know the contents of and a knife that is very clear in its purpose."

"A knife that I have purchased," Lord Richmond said slowly. "And a vial that I also have purchased."

A sudden fear clutched at Rebecca's heart. "Did you not say, Lord Richmond, that you were asked to go to various locations in town at certain times?" Seeing him nod, she closed her eyes. "And at each of those places, Lord Kensington was present?"

"He was, yes," Lord Richmond replied slowly. "Although I never once greeted him."

"But you *did* greet others who were present," Lord Swinton remarked, quickly becoming aware of what Rebecca meant. "They would know that you had been in the same vicinity as Lord Kensington."

"As though you were determined to remain near to him," Lady Hayward breathed, her eyes widening as she looked at Rebecca. "There is a plan here, Lord Richmond."

"A plan to have you embroiled in something so dreadful, I can hardly bear to speak of it," Rebecca continued, seeing the shock ripple across Lord Richmond's face as he came to understand what she meant. "*You* have followed Lord Kensington across London. *You* were the one who attempted to steal affections from his wife."

"And now, you are the one who has purchased a knife and a vial of some description," Lord Swinton finished as Lord Richmond set both hands down hard on the study table and leaned forward, his head bowed. "Quite what Lord Bellingham has to do with such things, however, I cannot say."

Lord Richmond blew out a long breath, and when he lifted his head to look at her, Rebecca could see the agony in his eyes.

"I am to be made out as the person responsible for Lord Kensington's demise," he said heavily. "That vial, no doubt, will be some concoction that will bring about either a deep sleep or his death."

"And the knife will be used and then left there, leaving Lady Kensington to cry and wail when she discovers him."

"And then to mention that the knife, she is sure, is yours, Lord Richmond," Lady Hayward continued, finishing off Lord Swinton's statement. "If anyone were to make particular inquiries, they would discover that you purchased both the knife and the vial."

Rebecca shuddered at the sheer horror of it all, seeing just how Lady Kensington had planned each and every step of her freedom. "No doubt, Lord Kensington will have made some arrangements for his wife, should he pass away before her."

"Which, of course," Lord Richmond muttered, "she will have made certain of." He let out a long breath and looked up at them all again. "Can we be certain of this? And what part does Lord Bellingham have in it all?"

Worrying her lip, Rebecca considered carefully, then looked up sharply.

"We must speak to Lord Kensington," she said as Lady Hayward caught her breath. "It is the only way to be certain of his safety, and that must be our priority at the present moment."

Lord Richmond began to nod but was quickly interrupted by Lord Swinton.

"Mayhap we will be able to do both," he said slowly. "We must speak to Lord Kensington, yes, but is there a way that we can have both Lord Bellingham and Lady Kensington join us when we do so?"

Rebecca waited, saying nothing as she looked from person to person. Lord Richmond was frowning hard, his brows low over his eyes, whilst Lady Hayward narrowed her eyes, staring down at the vial on the table.

"There is a ball in two days' time," Lady Hayward said eventually. "I am sure that Lord and Lady Kensington will attend. Lord Swinton, you would have to practically demand that Lord Kensington join you there. Quite how you would go about such a thing, I do not know."

"Then I would have to have Lady Kensington attend there also," Lord Richmond said slowly. "But if Lord Kensington is determined to keep his wife by his side, then what can we do to make certain that they attend separately?"

Lord Swinton chuckled. "Have no fear," he said as the others turned to watch him. "If Lady Kensington is dancing, shall we say, then I will be well able to convince Lord Kensington to join me for a short time." His smile faded. "I will speak of further rumors about his wife if I have to."

"Then," Rebecca said slowly, "if you are certain that Lord and Lady Kensington can be brought there, what of Lord Bellingham? We need him there also, do we not?" She looked around at the others and saw them all looking down at the vial and the knife, her stomach twisting as she allowed her gaze to linger there also.

"I will have to give the packages to Lord Bellingham," Lord Richmond said slowly. "It is expected of me."

"Then do so," Lord Swinton replied with a small, determined smile. "Tell him that you will be at Lord Gillingham's ball. The items can be placed in whatever room we will meet in, and he will have no concern about coming to speak to you. He is expecting the parcels, is he not?"

Lord Richmond nodded slowly, a look of relief wrapping across his expression. "Indeed, he is."

"And do you have any letters from Lady Kensington?" Rebecca asked quickly, her hopes fading as Lord Richmond looked away. "Do you mean to say you have not kept any of them?"

Lord Richmond let out a hard breath. "I have torn asunder or burned any she has sent me, out of both anger and frustration," he said heavily. "The only one I have remaining here at present is this one."

Trying to smile, Rebecca reached across and set her hand on his as it rested on the table, all too aware that Lady Hayward would be watching her closely.

"Then take that one," she said softly. "It will be enough."

"And Lady Kensington does not have to know that you have ripped or destroyed her other notes," Lord Swinton added as Rebecca murmured a quick agreement. "The shock of what you have either said or done might well be enough to frighten her into admitting it all."

"You will have saved Lord Kensington's life," Lady Hayward remarked as Rebecca smiled up into Lord Richmond's face, doing all she could to encourage him. "He will be inclined to listen to you."

"And perhaps," Rebecca murmured so that only he could hear, "Lord Kensington might be willing to state that all you have been accused of is quite unjust."

Lord Richmond let out a long breath. "I might be free of her and her duplicity for good," he said as Rebecca nodded, pulling her hand reluctantly away from his. "There is still a chance that..." He trailed off, but the words brought a fresh joy to Rebecca's heart, knowing what it was that he so desperately hoped for. She could not help but long for it too, knowing that it had been so far out of reach and now, suddenly, was just before them as though desperate to be found.

"Then this matter will soon come to a close, it seems,"

Lady Hayward remarked, looking at Rebecca with a smile. "Although we must all be prepared for what might occur. Lord Kensington might be unwilling to listen. Lady Kensington might deny it all, and her husband could well believe her."

Lord Richmond shook his head. "I am sure he will not, not once he hears the truth," he said firmly, his confidence filling Rebecca with hope. "It is time that all became clear, not only to us but to the *beau monde*. They should see Lady Kensington for who she truly is—a lady willing to manipulate and threaten those in her acquaintance simply so she might be able to gain for herself whatever she wishes. Even if it means the death of her husband."

A coldness ran down Rebecca's frame, but she pushed it away, determined to fill herself with nothing but courage and strength. "Then let us pray all goes well," she said quietly as Lord Richmond held her gaze, a hope burning in his eyes that Rebecca felt ignite in her soul. "So that true freedom might once more be found by you, Lord Richmond. For the good of us all."

CHAPTER THIRTEEN

"I have set both items aside in the room Lord Gillingham has granted us," Jeffery murmured as both he and Lord Swinton made their way slowly into the ballroom, the sound of music, conversation, and laughter rushing towards them like an overpowering wave. "He was most understanding."

Lord Swinton's brows rose. "You told him of your intention?"

Jeffery chuckled. "I was not at all specific, no," he said with a grin. "But I stated very clearly that it was to ensure that the life of one of his guests was not in any danger. That, certainly, piqued his curiosity, but he is too much of a gentleman to enquire further. Thus, we have been given a quiet parlor for our endeavors. There is a footman standing by the door so that you will know where to go."

Lord Swinton took in a long breath, no smile on his face this evening. "And you are quite certain that Lady Kensington will join you there?"

"*More* than certain," Jeffery replied with a rueful smile. "I will tell her that I intend to make for my estate come the morning and that I must discuss matters with her before I depart to make certain that she will do nothing more." He watched as the awareness of what such a thing would mean to Lady Kensington came into Lord Swinton's expression. "If I depart as planned, then she will not be able to do as she intends. Thus, she will, of course, say something to ensure I remain in London for a few days longer."

"Very good," Lord Swinton chuckled as Jeffery smiled wryly. "Then I hope this evening brings Lady Kensington's comeuppance. You deserve to be free of her, Richmond, and to be happy with another."

Jeffery lifted one eyebrow. "You mean Lady Rebecca."

"Of course, I mean Lady Rebecca!" Lord Swinton laughed as Jeffery allowed himself a broad smile of contentment. "She is clearly very dear to you, else you would not have had such a strong reaction to what you believed was the end of your acquaintance."

"I believe I have a deep affection for her," Jeffery replied honestly. "I have not yet fully examined my heart given all that has been happening, but, when it comes time to do so, I would not be surprised to discover that I love her."

Lord Swinton let out a sigh of satisfaction. "Then I shall be very glad to attend your wedding," he replied, making Jeffery laugh. "And I shall count myself responsible for your happiness."

"Let us hope it is as you say," Jeffery replied, his

stomach twisting as he caught sight of his quarry. "The evening, it seems, has begun."

~

"Lady Kensington."

Jeffery bowed and straightened, his whole body stiff with tension as she looked back at him, her eyes gleaming with evident delight at his discomfort. Quickly greeting the rest of the group that stood together, Jeffery forced himself to take in deep, slow breaths. He knew what he had to say for Lady Kensington to take note of his intentions, but to do so immediately would not be wise. Allowing the conversation to flow around him and fully aware that he was receiving some dark looks from some of those in the small group, Jeffery cleared his throat and swung his arms behind his back, his hands clasping together.

"It is interesting that you speak of missing the country, Lord Birchall," he said, looking at the gentleman rather than at Lady Kensington. "I, myself, intend to return to my country estate rather than remain in London."

Another gentleman chortled. "Then you have been chased away, Lord Richmond!"

Bristling, Jeffery tried to keep his irritation hidden, shrugging instead. "I am tired of London," he said calmly. "That is all."

Lady Kensington said nothing, but, as Jeffery allowed his gaze to pass over the group, he saw the paleness in her face and the way her lips had flattened from her confident smile. Evidently, he had worried her.

"When do you depart?" asked another gentleman, and Jeffery gave him a small smile.

"Tomorrow," he said as a few murmurs of surprise came up from those listening. "As soon as I am ready, I shall be gone from London, and I confess that nothing can convince me otherwise." Clearing his throat again, he looked past Lady Kensington, pretending to see someone else. "Oh, if you will excuse me." Taking his leave, he walked away from the group, a broad smile on his face, knowing that he would soon have Lady Kensington seeking him out to discuss all she could with him.

∽

"I HAVE no reason to speak with you!"

Jeffery glared at Lady Kensington as she drew near to him, beckoning him towards her.

"You will, Lord Richmond," she said sharply. "My husband has allowed me a few moments of freedom—although quite where he has gone, I do not know—and I *will* speak with you."

Jeffery snorted and shook his head. "I have no reason to do so, as I have said," he stated, turning on his heel. "You said that this was all at an end, that you would demand nothing more of me. You cannot expect me to remain in your company, particularly when you have already driven me out of London!"

Lady Kensington laughed harshly, the sound grating on Jeffery's nerves.

"You will do what I ask for as long as you remain in London, Lord Richmond," she told him sharply. "Lady Rebecca is still within your affections, I am sure of it, and you know full well what I can do if you do not comply."

Making a show of being more than frustrated at Lady Kensington's demands, Jeffery eventually allowed himself to concede, stating that they would have to find a private room to discuss anything she wished, for fear of being overheard or seen. A few quick arrangements and Jeffery stalked through the ballroom and towards the parlor where he hoped Lord Kensington and Lord Swinton were already waiting. Lady Kensington, he knew, would follow after him soon.

His breathing quickening, Jeffery pushed open the door of the parlor, murmuring to the footman to allow one Lady Kensington entry, should she come in search of him. Stepping inside, he let his breath rattle out of him, seeing Lord Kensington and Lord Swinton sitting by the fireplace, although Lord Kensington's face darkened instantly.

"Lord Kensington," Jeffery said quickly. "Please, I know that you think very poorly of me, but I have arranged for you to be here to protect your very life."

Lord Kensington said nothing, although his frown lifted just a little. Glancing at Lord Swinton and seeing him nod, he turned back to Jeffery.

"I have no particular interest in whatever you are speaking of," Lord Kensington said suddenly, rising to his feet. "I do not trust you, Lord Richmond and I—"

The door behind Jeffery swung open and, much to his relief, in stepped Lady Hayward and Lady Rebecca.

"Oh, you are here!" Lady Hayward said as Lady Rebecca came to stand directly beside him. "I am glad. I have given Lady Anna and Lady Selina into the care of my dear friend Lady Cartwright, but I cannot be absent for long."

"I was just taking my leave," Lord Kensington said stiffly, giving Lady Hayward a short bow. "If you will excuse me."

Lady Rebecca stepped forward before anyone else could speak.

"Pray, do not," she said softly, her eyes searching Lord Kensington's. "It is of the utmost importance that you remain. Truly, Lord Kensington. Your life is in danger."

The gentleman laughed harshly at this, scoffing the remark, but the rest of the group remained entirely silent. The sound died away, and Jeffery could see the way Lord Kensington's certainty began to fade. His eyes darted from one person to the next, looking hard at Jeffery for some moments.

"It will be quite painful," Jeffery said quietly. "It will cause you trouble to hear what I have to say, Lord Kensington, but it is for the best." Knowing that Lady Kensington was soon to join them, he spread his hands. "Your wife, Lady Kensington, has been doing all she can to manipulate me. She has threatened Lady Rebecca's reputation, Lord Swinton's reputation, as well as others that I consider my friends."

Lord Kensington threw up his hands. "You can hardly expect me to believe this!" he exclaimed, his eyes wide. "You might very well have convinced others, but I shall not believe it."

"You must," Lord Swinton told him sternly. "It is well known amongst the *ton* that your wife is something of a flirt, Lord Kensington. You know it well, I am sure, but you continue to deny it to yourself. Will you truly continue to do so now when your life might be in danger?"

Lord Kensington made to speak, only to close his mouth tightly again. He shook his head fervently, but no sound came out, as though he were attempting to convince himself that he was right in his own mind. Jeffery prayed that it was not so.

"What is it that my wife has supposedly done?" Lord Kensington asked sharply, looking up at Jeffery. "Why do you believe her to be so malicious?"

Jeffery opened his mouth to reply, only for the door to open again and, with a look of shock rippling across her features, Lady Kensington to step inside. Her hand remained on the door handle, the door wide open, but with one swift action, Lady Hayward stepped back and swiftly closed it, wrenching it from Lady Kensington's hand. With a sense of satisfaction, Jeffery looked back at Lord Kensington and saw the heavy frown begin to settle over his features as he looked at his wife. He too saw the wide eyes, the paleness that had shot into her cheeks, and the worry now playing about her mouth.

"Lady Kensington," Jeffery said softly. "I have just informed your husband of the threats you have settled over me, forcing me to do as you ask. He has not believed me thus far, but it does not matter, for I will soon be able to prove it." Clearing his throat, he looked back to Lord Kensington. "Lord Kensington, your wife first informed me that I was to make arrangements with one Lord Bellingham on her behalf, given that she could not do so herself since you were watching her with a sharp eye. Lord Bellingham was to call upon your wife during the fashionable hour when you were absent, which I believe he did." Taking in a deep breath and seeing Lady Kensington sinking into a chair, Jeffery continued with determination. "Thereafter, she gave me a series of appointments I was to fulfill. I had to visit various places in London and, much to my astonishment, at each time, you were there also."

Lord Kensington sucked in a breath, looking wide-eyed at his wife. "You have been very interested in my plans of late," he said, his words hard and cold. "I have thought it an attempt to show interest in me, but it seems I was wrong."

"I did not understand why such a thing occurred, nor why I had to greet another gentleman present at the time, but I could not refuse for fear of what would occur if I did not." He felt Lady Rebecca's hand slip into his and squeezed it gently, all the more grateful for her support. "I have come to care very deeply for Lady Rebecca, and your wife, being aware of my feelings, did whatever she could to use it against me. Therefore, I asked no questions when I was told to purchase items that had already been set aside for me. I had to do this on two separate occasions, Lord Kensington, and I did so without hesitation. I did not, however, untie the string and look inside these parcels, again, out of fear as to what would occur with Lady Rebecca if I did so. That is, until two days ago, when Lord Swinton, Lady Rebecca, and

Lady Hayward stood with me, and we all found out what was inside."

"This is nonsense!" Lady Kensington cried, her hands flying up around her ears as she gesticulated wildly. "There is no need to listen to such ravings, Lord Kensington. We should return to the ballroom and leave Lord Richmond alone. He has gone quite mad and appears quite determined to—"

"Lady Kensington, I believe that Lord Richmond was to give these parcels to Lord Bellingham," Lady Rebecca interrupted, her voice flooding the room as Lady Kensington stared back at her, her face milk-white. "Lord Bellingham is to come and collect them from this very room. He will be able to confirm what Lord Richmond has said."

"Besides which," Jeffery continued softly, "I have a note here. A note that you wrote to me, demanding that I do the very thing you have just refuted." Pulling it from his pocket, he handed it to Lord Kensington, who took it with a shaking hand. Jeffery did not like upsetting the gentleman, but he knew the truth had to be revealed. "The parcels, Lord Kensington, contained a knife and a vial."

Lord Kensington lifted his head from where he was reading the note and stared at Jeffery, despair beginning to fill his eyes. "A vial?"

"We do not know what it is," Lord Swinton said quietly, "but we have concluded that Lady Kensington is planning your death, Lord Kensington. And, given that Lord Richmond will have been seen following you around London, given that society believes him to be guilty of attempting to steal your wife's affections, guilt will, of course, instantly be pushed onto him."

"And, in addition," Lady Hayward said quietly, "he has been the one to purchase both the knife and the vial. The shopkeepers will testify to it, and I do not doubt that Lady Kensington would make certain they were given the opportunity to do so."

Jeffery took in a deep breath. "Which means, Lord Kensington, that I would be given yet more unearned guilt, although this time it would be a much more grievous matter," he said as Lord Kensington dropped his head, his breath rushing out of him. "But whilst I fear for myself, Lord Kensington, my concern is also for you."

"As it was for all of us," Lady Hayward remarked. "Your wife is attempting to remove you from this earth, Lord Kensington, so she might have both financial and social freedom."

Lord Kensington closed his eyes tightly, his shoulders slumping as he dropped his head. "I have made arrangements for my wife to be financially secure should I pass before her," he said, his voice broken with emotion. "If this is true..."

"It is not!" Lady Kensington cried, throwing herself out of her chair and hurrying towards her husband. "Please, Kensington, do not believe a word of this!"

"I have the items here," Jeffery said, letting go of Lady Rebecca's hand and going to retrieve them from where he had placed them earlier. "And as I have said, Lord Bellingham—"

Before he could say another word, the door opened again, and Lord Bellingham stepped inside. His eyes flared wide in a moment, but, for what was now the second time, Lady Hayward stepped neatly past and closed the door tightly.

"Lord Bellingham," Jeffery said, straightening. "Lord Kensington has some questions for you. Questions I will not ask myself for fear of influencing the outcome, but I would beg of you to answer honestly." He picked up the two wrapped items and set them down in front of Lord Kensington, who looked from Lord Bellingham to the parcels and then back again. "You might begin by stating whether or not you are aware of what is within these parcels."

Making his way back to Lady Rebecca, he stood with her, one hand settling around her waist as she leaned into him. The warmth of her was reassuring, the strength of her comfort in simply being present bore him on as Lord Kensington began to ask Lord Bellingham about what he had done.

The man looked utterly terrified. His eyes were wide, his hands shaking, and his voice quavered whenever he spoke. Every so often, he would look to Lady Kensington, but she would look away, turning her head as though she did not even wish to see him.

"You were to do as my wife asked you?" Lord Kensington said as Lord Bellingham swallowed visibly. "Why?"

"She..." Lord Bellingham trembled. "She promised me that I would be rewarded for such loyalty," he said, his cheeks now crimson as the meaning of his words became clear to them all. "That was our first meeting. I—I did not know the extent of what she meant, but I was willing to do as she asked." Dropping his head with evident shame, he lowered his voice. "I was then to collect some items from Lord Richmond and bring them to her the next time she sent for me."

"And do you know what these items are?" Lord Kensington asked, picking up the first and opening it, the paper ripping under his hands. "Have you any knowledge of what is within them?"

Lord Bellingham shook his head but did not look at Lord Kensington. "I do not, my lord," he said pathetically.

No one spoke. Lady Kensington let out a soft moan and moved to sit down again, her fear and upset palpable, but no one gave her any attention. Instead, they watched as Lord Kensington revealed first the vial, then the knife.

Jeffery said nothing, his heart thumping furiously as Lord Kensington set the two items back down on the table and then, with a deep breath, looked directly at him.

"The night you were at my soiree, Lord Richmond," he said heavily. "I knew very well that my wife had sought you out. I had seen her attempt to do so before, and I had seen your response to her. You were not as eager to chase after her as she hoped."

Beside him, Jeffery heard Lady Rebecca gasp, although, much to his relief, she said nothing.

"I am all too aware of my wife's foibles," Lord Kensington continued, throwing his wife a dark look. "But I never once expected her to attempt to do something as treacherous as this."

Lady Kensington shuddered violently, now a crumpled heap in her chair, but Jeffery felt no sympathy for her. She had brought this on herself, and whatever consequences lay before her now were of her own making.

"I am sorry that I allowed society to believe that you were pursuing my wife," Lord Kensington continued, his expression grave and his words heavy with emotion. "I will right such a rumor, Lord Richmond. You have my word." Lifting his chin just a little, he held out one hand towards him. "And thank you for what you have done."

Jeffery stepped forward and grasped Lord Kensington's hand firmly, thinking to himself that it appeared the man had aged heavily in the last few minutes. "Thank you, Lord Kensington," he said quietly. "I would be very grateful for such an action."

Lord Kensington nodded, then turned to his wife, who looked up at him with terrified eyes. Jeffery, seeing Lady Hayward making for the door, grasped Lady Rebecca's hand and followed out after her, leaving Lord Bellingham and Lord Swinton to bring up the rear. The door closed behind Lord Swinton, and, with that, the dreadful affair was over.

EPILOGUE

"And you are quite sure about him, Father?"

The duke looked up from his papers, having dismissed Rebecca only a few moments before. As she had walked away, another niggle of uncertainty had bitten at her, and she had been forced to return. Her father, however, did not appear to be at all exasperated. Instead, he gave her a small smile, tilting his head just a little as he did so.

"I am not about to change my mind, Rebecca," he said firmly. "Lady Hayward has made certain that the rumors are unfounded. I have looked into the gentleman thoroughly and am quite satisfied. And, if I were not," he continued, a twinkle in his eye, "then I would not have given him permission to court you."

A delighted smile spread across Rebecca's face as she clasped her hands together tightly. Lord Richmond would call at any moment, and she was overwhelmed with both excitement and hope. "Thank you, Father," she said, seeing him nod but then immediately pick up his papers again. Stepping out, she closed the door tightly and then leaned back against it for a moment, her fingers at her chin and her eyes closing as she dragged in air.

It had been a sennight since they had all managed to speak to Lord Kensington. A sennight since Lord Kensington had made the promise to remove all trace of guilt from Lord Richmond, and in that time, he had done precisely that. Lord Kensington had removed himself and his wife from London, had stated, quite clearly, to those near to him that he knew now that Lord Richmond had done nothing wrong and that, much to the *ton*'s shock, his wife was the one who had behaved inappropriately. The shock of his statements had run through society like wildfire, and Rebecca had been more than relieved when Lord Richmond was finally welcomed back into society without hesitation.

It had meant Lady Hayward recommending to the duke that a courtship be allowed to take place between Rebecca and Lord Richmond, and now, finally, it seemed that he had agreed.

Making her way to the drawing-room, her excitement building with every step, Rebecca felt her heart quickening with the joy that would soon be hers. Lord Richmond was the only gentleman who had captured her interest, and now, she had to admit, her heart.

"Oh, my lady!"

Rebecca looked up to see the butler nearing the drawing-room, with Lord Richmond in his wake.

"Lord Richmond has come to call," the butler said, gesturing to him. "I shall send for a tea tray."

Rebecca nodded, warmth hitting her cheeks as she

looked at Lord Richmond. "Lady Hayward is to arrive also," she called after the butler, aware of just how soft her voice was. "She is tardy, I believe, but will be here presently."

Lord Richmond chuckled and, pushing open the drawing room door, held it back for her.

"I do hope she is tardy purposefully," he said with such meaning that Rebecca felt a tremor run down her spine. "I have longed for only a few minutes alone with you."

Following after her but making sure to leave the door ajar, Lord Richmond let out a long breath and held out his hands to her. Gladly, Rebecca took them at once, stepping close to him and lifting her face to his.

"I am accepted by your father, it seems," he murmured as she smiled up at him. "He has said that I might ask you something particular."

"Oh?" Her heart was beating so loudly, she was certain he could hear it, and yet she wanted to be nowhere other than in his arms.

His expression changed, the smile fading as he lifted one hand and brushed his hand down her cheek, cupping her chin gently. "You must know, Lady Rebecca, that when I ask you this, I ask it because of what I hope for." His eyes seemed to glow with life, his lips lifting slightly as he held her gaze. "I ask it because I hope for a future with you. A future that speaks of love and joy and all manner of happiness. You have quite captured my heart, Lady Rebecca. I have never known another like you. From the very first moment, you saw my heart, saw the truth that so many did not, and you clung to it. Without your determination, I do not think I would have ever escaped from Lady Kensington. And now, here I stand before you, free of rumor, free of scandal, and free to love you as my heart so desperately desires."

Rebecca could not speak for some moments, trying to take in what he had said and finding her heart so overcome with all manner of emotion that she simply could not think of what to say. His fingers were gentle on her skin, his other hand pressing her fingers lightly. There was no fear or doubt in his heart or his expression any longer. There was nothing to hold either of them back, nothing to push them asunder, and Rebecca reveled in that freedom.

"My dear Richmond," she murmured, placing her free hand lightly on his chest, next to his heart. "I recall the day we met. I recall it with such clarity that I remember all that I felt. Something within me drew near to you, and I could not remove you from my thoughts. Since then, my heart has found itself yearning for you, Lord Richmond. I have felt despair, loss, brokenness, and joy. Now that I know there is nothing further to prevent our happiness, my heart is so overcome with love that I do not know how to express it."

Lord Richmond smiled, his hands slipping about her waist. "I believe I do," he murmured, the look in his eyes making her heart race as he lowered his head, his lips finding hers in a gentle kiss.

Rebecca responded to him at once, her whole being filled with such extraordinary sensations that she found herself clinging to him as though he were the very air she needed to breathe. When he lifted his head, Rebecca kept her eyes closed, steadying herself for a few moments before she allowed herself to look back at him.

He was still smiling.

"You will accept my court, will you not?" he asked quietly. "You know my heart. You know my intention. Will you be my own sweet wife, Lady Rebecca?"

Joy overflowed within her. "My dear Jeffery," she whispered, her happiness now complete. "Of course I will."

I HOPE you enjoyed Rebecca and Jeffrey's story! I was happy to see Lord Richmond get out of his situation with the help of his friends! The next book in the series is still a work in process!

Please check out the first book in The Spinster's Guild series A New Beginning or check out all of my books on Amazon! Rose Pearson

Printed in Dunstable, United Kingdom